THE FIRST FAST DRAW

THE FIRST FAST DRAW

DRAW

LOUIS L'AMOUR

BANTAM BOOKS

NEW YORK · TORONTO · LONDON · SYDNEY · AUCKLAND

THE FIRST FAST DRAW
A Literary Express, Inc. Book
(a subsidiary of Doubleday Direct, Inc.)
Published in arrangement with
Bantam Books, Inc.
1540 Broadway
New York, NY 10036

PRINTING HISTORY

Bantam rack-size edition/February 1959
Louis L'Amour Hardcover Collection/June 1998

If you want to purchase more of these titles, please write to:
The Louis L'Amour Collection
1540 Broadway
New York, NY 10036

ISBN: 1-58165-049-3

Published simultaneously in the United States and Canada

PRINTED IN THE UNITED STATES OF AMERICA

THE FIRST FAST DRAW

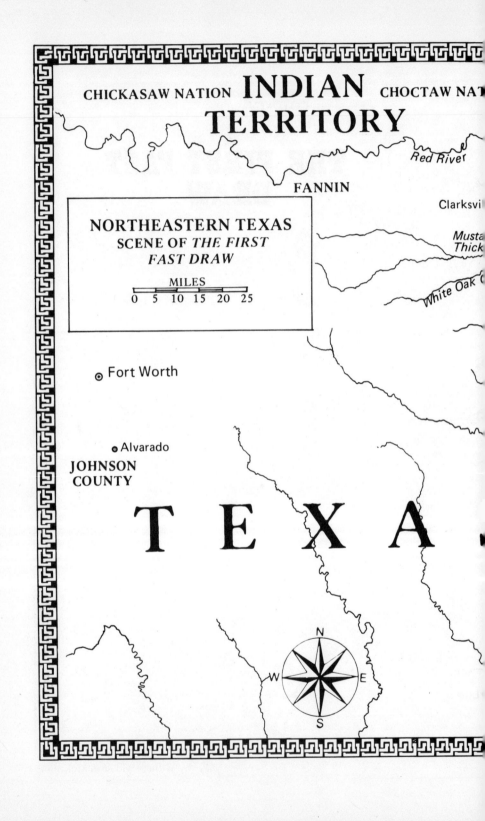

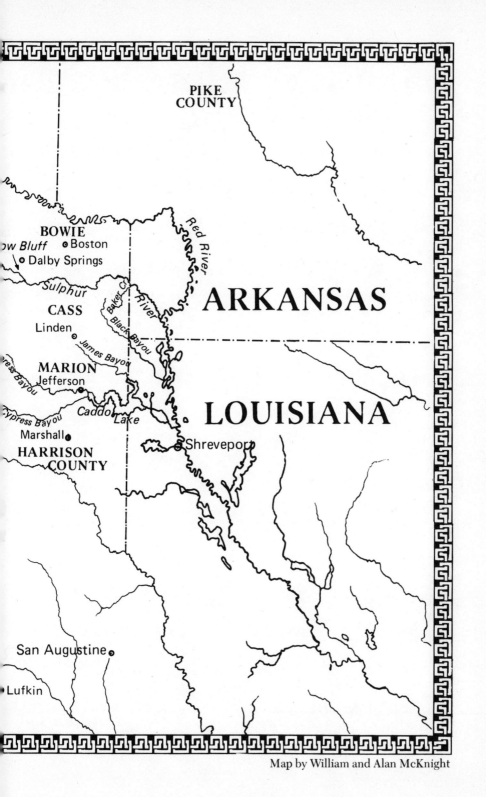

PIKE
COUNTY

BOWIE
w Bluff ○Boston
Dalby Springs

Sulphur

Red River

Baker Cr.

River

Black Bayou

ARKANSAS

CASS
Linden

James Bayou

MARION
Jefferson

ess Bayou

Cypress Bayou Caddo Lake

Marshall

HARRISON
COUNTY

LOUISIANA

Shreveport

San Augustine ○

Lufkin

Map by William and Alan McKnight

ONE

When the shelter was finished, thatched heavy with pine boughs, I went inside and built myself a hatful of fire. It was a cold, wet, miserable time, and nowhere around any roof for me, although here I was, back in my own country.

Hungry I was, and soaked to the hide from a fall my mule had taken in the swamp, but I kept my fire small, for I'd come home by the back trails, figuring to attract no notice until I could look around and take stock.

They'd given me nothing here in the old days, and I'd given them a sight less, and the only memory they would have of me would be one of violence and anger. Yet hereabouts was all I had ever known of home, or was likely to know.

The woods dripped with rain. Sometimes a big drop would fall from the thatch overhead and hiss in the fire, but other than that and the soft fall of rain in the twilight forest, there was no sound. Not at first.

When a sound did come it was faint. But it was not a sound of the forest, nor of the rain, nor of any wild animal or bird, for these were sounds I knew and had known since childhood.

1

It was a rider coming, maybe two, and nobody I wanted to see, but that was why I'd put together my lean-to back over the knoll and hid down deep among the rain-wet trees.

This was a rider coming and I could only hope the rain had left no trail they could find, for if trouble was to come to me here, I wanted it to wait, at least until I had walked the old path to the well again, and seen where Pa was buried.

Standing there like that with the rain dripping down, me in my shabby homespun, wore-out clothes, I tried to figure if there was anybody hereabouts beyond a few Caddos whom I could call friend. I couldn't think of anybody.

For a long time then there was no other sound but the rain, a whisper of rain falling among the leaves, and a far-off stirring of wind. And then I heard that sound again.

Behind me the raw-boned mule lifted his head and pricked his ears against the sound, so it wasn't only me heard the sound. No matter, the buckskin mule was ga'nted some and it would be a few days of rest he'd need before I could move on anyway, and maybe I just wasn't feeling right to move at all. Maybe I had come home to stay . . . whether they liked it or not.

Rising, I could just see across the top of the knoll in the forest, and the place I'd chosen to camp commanded a view of the trail at intervals along its course through the swamp woods.

When at last they came in sight there were two riders and they rode as tired men ride, and there was that about them that was somehow familiar. Maybe it was only that they were mighty near as shabby as me, unkempt and lonely as me.

Two riders walking their horses, two riders hunting something. That something could be me.

My Spencer carbine was behind me and so I reached a hand back for it and pulled it close against my side for shelter from the rain. It was a new Spencer, caliber .56 and she carried seven shots—I'd picked it off a dead man up in the Nation. A brand-new, spanking-new, mighty slick piece of shooting iron.

Right there I stood with no notion of moving. Place I stood was a hidden place where a body might pass within six feet and never see it was there. Man like me, in unfriendly country, he can't be too careful. These past years I had seen almost nothing but unfriendly country. Maybe it was my own fault, for I was a man rode careful and who kept a gun to hand.

When I saw them first through the farthest gap in the trees, I'd seen nothing but a couple of men hunched in their saddles, one wearing a ragged poncho, the other a gray Confederate greatcoat.

A moment only, a glimpse, and then they were gone from sight among the trees that lined the trail below, but at the nearest point they would be no more than thirty yards away. So I waited where I was, trusting not to be seen, but keeping the Spencer to hand in case of trouble.

This was a place I knew, an arm of the swamp to protect my right flank, an almost impassable thicket of brush on my left, and the main swamp close in behind me. There was a trail came from the swamp into the trees behind me, but anyone using that trail was likely to be a Caddo or someone as averse to trouble as myself.

The brush on my left could be got through, no question of that, but not without a sight more noise than anybody was likely to make, coming easy to a strange camp.

The people of this northeast corner of Texas had not liked me before, and with times what they were they had no reason to be friendly. The War between the States was just over a few days past, and it was a wary time for strangers.

In the old days when a boy I'd taken nothing from them, nor given them anything they could lay hold on, they disliked me from the start because I wouldn't knuckle under to the town boys, and I'd met dislike with dislike, anger with anger, fist with fist. Despite the war that intervened they would not have forgotten.

Yet it was to this land that I'd come home, for it was as much

3

of a home as I could claim, and despite the hard ways of the people toward me, it was a land I loved. From the deep silences of the forgotten swamp lagoons to the stillness of the fields at evening with the mist of night laying low along the fences, it was a place that belonged to me. There was a feel of things growing here, of a rich, dark soil bursting with eagerness to grow beneath my feet.

Those riders came along . . . there was something seemed familiar about them, but this corner of Texas had been a bloody country filled with black angers and feuding families, and now to the old hatreds there would be added the feeling left by the war just now ended. It was no country for a man to step out and go hailing strangers—least of all for me.

My tiny fire was over the top of the knoll from them and behind a great dead log, the side of the log serving as a reflector to throw heat back into the lean-to. It was snug and tight, and should have been, for I'd lived most of my life like this, and it was most two years since I'd slept beneath a roof of any decent kind. What little smoke the fire gave off lost itself among the leaves overhead, yet a knowing man with a keen nose might catch a whiff if the wind was right.

They drew up in the trail below, in plain sight and an easy shot for my rifle, and they talked there, and one of their voices had an old, familiar ring. So I stepped out of my shelter and strolled down the slope of the knoll toward them, walking soft on the dead wet leaves underfoot. The carbine was in my right hand and in my belt was a Dragoon Colt, within easy grasping.

"Bob Lee," I said aloud, and no louder than needed.

They turned sharp around, but it was to the more slender of the two whom I spoke. He looked at me, measuring me, then making up his mind.

What he was seeing wasn't much. A battered black slouch hat, a shabby buckskin jacket, squaw-made by a Ute west of the big mountains, with cabin-spun shirt and pants, mighty worn. My boots were Army issue, and the man in them a lean,

4

dark young man standing two inches more than six feet in his socks, and weighing nigh two hundred pounds, but with the face of a man who had known much trouble and little of softness or loving—the face of a man born to struggle and the hard ways.

"Cullen, is it? Damn it, man, it's been years!"

"Three."

"I'd have guessed it longer. Bill Longley, meet Cullen Baker, such a man as we need right now in this country."

"I'll take no man's word for that," I said. "They'd no use for me before."

"You were a hard lad, Cullen. And once the trouble began you believed we were all against you, all over the five counties."

"Coffee yonder." I turned away, walking back up the knoll not wanting them to see how it moved me, the friendly way of them to a man just back in his own country, but where he'd expected nothing.

Bob Lee was a gentleman, a man of some book learning, a thin-faced man, and proud. He came of a family known in the South and respected, and the temper he had along with his skill with weapons and readiness to use them won him another kind of respect from another kind of man. Yet whatever anybody said of Bob Lee, nobody said anything except that he was an honorable man.

Bill Longley? He was eighteen then, a tall, raw-boned young man who in his time was to be known as one of the most feared of Texas pistol fighters, but that time was yet to come, and I'd only heard his name first up in the Nation, and I could not remember what had been said of him.

Hunkered down beside the fire, I stirred the coals and got out my cup. Each of them dug a blackened cup from among his gear and we shared the coffee in my beat-up old pot. Long ago Pa taught me to share what I had with guests if it was the last I had, although few had done the same for me.

"You're returning at a black time, Cullen. The Reconstruc-

tion people are in, confiscating property and raising hob generally with anyone who fought for the South. If they've not taken
your place already, they'll be after it."

"They will buy trouble, then."

"Trouble is what they want, I'm afraid. They have the Army
here, and more of it coming, and they've friends from about
here to tell them the choice land."

"You've got to jump to their tune or you'll have to fight,"
Longley said.

"I've had enough of fighting," I replied. "I want no more of
trouble from any man."

"Your wishes won't chop much cotton, Cullen. If you have
what they want, they'll take it. And if you don't accept their
rule with a tight mouth, you'll have trouble." Bob Lee glanced
at me. "It has come to me already."

Rain fell among the leaves, and I'd a sorrow on me, and a
deepening fury, too. Could a man not be left alone? There had
been small chance in the old days for me to be anything but a
bad one, although the Good Lord knows I'd wasted little time
waiting for the invitation. When they came to me with trouble
in those years, I was out there to meet them halfway.

A boy can be that way, but I was a man grown now, with a
man's hard judgment, and some long miles behind me of riding
with a gun for companion, through bitter, lonely days and
more miles than I rightly could remember.

There was deep within me a love of the land, of a rich soil
and what a man could grow, and over all those dry miles in the
West I'd thought of the greens and beauties of this corner of
Texas. I was back wanting no troubles left over from a war I'd
never fought, nor had sympathy for, on either side.

Longley brought fuel to the fire and went off into the dark to
strip the gear from the two horses and bring it under the
shelter. Under the branches of the huge cypress where I'd
picketed my mule there was room enough for a dozen horses,

and mighty little rain came through the thick tangle of Spanish moss, leaves and branches. The horses would be dry enough.

The coffee smelled good, and the sound of rain was friendly now. Sitting there smelling the coffee I got to thinking how strange it was that Bob Lee, of all folks, should be a friend of mine. Not that we'd ever been close, only from the first he'd seemed to understand me. Maybe it was because we'd both had our fighting troubles.

Only he had education. His folks had wealth, and many friends. Time to time I'd heard talk of him during the War—he'd become a colonel, and a good officer. Now that he was home I could see it would not be easy for him with his fine pride, and even less easy for me.

Folks would not have forgotten Cullen Baker. They would remember, and that was handicap enough without trouble shaping up with Reconstruction soldiers and carpetbaggers. The ones from Texas could be the worst, poor whites and such; now they had their chance to strut and talk up, they'd use it.

All the way home I'd seen them coming like locusts into a cornfield, the poor kind of men quick to jump on the band wagon once they'd heard the music and knew which way the parade was going. In every community there are those quick to take advantage, just as there are those who have no loyalty except to their property and their skin's safety.

Sitting there, huddled over our small fire, we yarned the hours away, with Bob Lee telling about the war and the State of Texas, and what had happened and what he figured was going to happen. None of it shaped up as likely for a man named Cullen Baker, who'd be caught fair in the middle.

I'd no family awaiting me. Ma died long ago when I was a youngster, and Pa died while I was gone west. Nobody cared whether I came or went, but here I owned property, and here I aimed to stay, to raise me a crop, and to try to make something of myself.

This time I'd try to make it different than when we first came

7

down from Tennessee. Maybe I could have avoided the first trouble, but I was a youngster then, and too proud. A really tough man never has to prove anything to anybody, he knows what he can do and he doesn't care even a mite whether anybody else knows or not. With a youngster it's otherwise. He figures he's got to show everybody how tough he is or nobody will believe it, so he winds up in plenty of grief.

When the Civil War broke out I was west of the Rockies. When most folks got worked up about it the whole shebang seemed far away and mighty unreasonable to me, and I couldn't get wrought up. Never being sure which side was right I lost no sleep over it, and out there in Utah it seemed far away. When I did come east it seemed that being from the South I should join up, and Quantrill being the nearest to me, I joined his outfit.

From the first I didn't shape up with that crowd. They were a lot of murdering, drunken thieves, burning down farms or attacking unarmed folks—didn't seem right to me. I had come east to fight a war, not to rape farm women and burn barns. Right after the first shindig I decided I'd bought myself a ticket on the wrong train.

Cap'n Weaver—he was my boss with that outfit—was a thick-set man with a rust-red beard and a blustering loud-mouthed way about him. He shaped up like a man who was all noise and bluster, and no kind of man in a scrap. He had with him a kid horse thief they called Dingus who had a Bible-toting brother. I liked none of them.

Morning after that fight I rode up to Weaver. "I don't like this outfit. I'm riding out."

He set there staring at me and those two brothers they set there, and then Weaver says, "You can't go nowhere thout permission, an' permission you ain't about to git."

"Ain't asked for it. I'm just a-leaving. I don't cotton to the way you do things in this outfit, destroying crops, burning up farms, and attacking womenfolks. I worked to raise a few crops myself and I won't have no part of such carryin' on."

Well, sir, his face was a sight. Behind those dirty whiskers he began to swell up and flush up red like a country girl caught in the back of a farm wagon with a boy. There for a minute I thought he'd bust a gut. Then he spoke up real big. "You got two minutes to git where you b'long or you'll be court-martialed for refusin' duty."

Most accidental-like my carbine was lyin' across my saddle and pointed right at his heart, and my hand was right over the trigger guard. But I wasn't leaving those brothers out of my sight, either. "You better get on with whatever you've a might to do," I told him, "or I won't be around to see the fun."

Weaver, he made a start for a gun but the *click* of that cocking Spencer stopped him. I never did figure him to have belly enough to stand up to a man. "Now you looka here!" he began to loud-mouth it. "You cain't—"

"I already have," I told him, and rode out of camp.

Of course, once I had the camp behind me I lit out of there like who flung the chunk, and when I was well down the trail I lost my tracks in those of the night before, and then cut off across the country.

That was miles ago and weeks ago, and now I was back, almost within hollering distance of the home where I was brought up, the only one I could rightly recall.

Not that it had ever mattered to anybody but me. Those days I was a lonely youngster, shabbier than anybody else and too proud to try to make friends after that first trouble. That was why I started going to the swamp. When a man has no friends he makes up for it sometimes by learning a lot, and I learned a-plenty in those Sulphur River bottoms, and knew all that country away down to Caddo Lake. I knew places even the Caddo Indians didn't know.

Those days I wandered the swamp trails, hunted and trapped for fur, and I knew where the solid ground was, and the passages a man could go through in a dugout canoe, and the hide-outs of the Indians and a few runaway slaves.

Now I was back. The farm would be there; most folks called it a ranch. There would still be the orchard and the cabin would be standing, and there was land belonging to me that stretched away down to the Big Thicket. Only those days land was not worth much, and everybody had a-plenty of it.

Lying awake staring up into the dark where the rain dripped from the cypress trees, it felt good to be back home. There was nobody anywhere who cared whether I came or went, but I knew the soil, and I knew what I could do with it, given a chance. And I'd been as homeless as a worn-out saddle pony for so long.

My plans were clear and proud. First off I'd break ground and put in a crop, and once I'd earned some cash from selling my crop I'd buy a brood mare and start raising blooded horses. Maybe a man could find a stallion with good lines; there was money to be made with a well-bred stallion.

As a boy in those East Texas swamps and thickets I'd almost never seen anything like a really good horse. Of course, there were some good horses around, but not much of it ever came my way and the horses folks up there had were a rugged bunch, tough stock, and good for working cattle in the brush, but I wanted some horses.

Time had been, right after I took off from home, I'd gone north through Virginia and Kentucky. Talk about horses.

Most of the breeders in the South had been put out of business by the war, so a man with a good stallion, good mares and pasture, a man set up like that could do all right.

Boylike, I'd figured to be rich some time. Every boy at one time or another wants to be rich. He wants to strut it around and make smart with the best clothes and have the girls look him over. He figures with enough money showing the girls will all get round heels when he comes around.

One thing I'd learned was it mattered mighty little how

10

much money a man had as long as he was contented. Me, I wanted enough to eat, my own roof to sleep under, and my own place with crops and horses growing.

Some time maybe I'd find me a woman. Not in this country. I'd go away for that. Hereabouts the name of Cullen Baker was a bad name and nobody was likely to want me.

There would be trouble enough, but trouble begins with people and I would stay shut of them. None of them had any use for me, anyway, and that would make it a simple thing. Run down the way the place was sure to be, I'd have my work cut out for me without traipsing off to town, tomcatting around and maybe getting my tail in a crack.

Longley got up quietly when I figured he was asleep, and rustled an armful of dry wood. If a man can find dry wood after three days of rain he's a man to ride the river with.

Bob Lee turned over and sat up, reaching for his pipe.

Longley squatted over the fire. "Seems quiet," he said. "Bob, you reckon them carpetbaggers from up the state at Boston will come into the swamps hunting us?"

"Not unless they're crazier'n they look." Bob Lee turned to me. "You awake, Cullen? We should have explained it to you. We had a difficulty up to Boston. Shot a man."

"Needed it, I reckon. You always were a proud man, Bob Lee, but I never knew you to shoot too quick nor to kill a man who wasn't asking for it."

We talked it over some, and they told me more about the country I'd come back to, and none of it looked very good for my plans. There was one thing they forgot to tell me, but I learned it soon enough: my worst enemy was back there, and he was a big man around the country. He was a Southern man but he was thick with carpetbaggers. I would never have believed it of him.

Some time about then we all went to sleep. Bob Lee was right. Any carpetbagger who followed them into the swamps would be crazy. Both men were tired, like men are who have

spent sleepless nights of running and riding, and if a man like
Bob Lee could be on the dodge, with folks everywhere around,
how could I hope to stick it out?

Nobody talked much when we saddled up come daylight. I
told them about the trail into the Sulphur Swamps. Unless you
know it, I'll tell you. That Sulphur is a might twisty stream,
and there's bayous running off from it and a good bit of swamp,
and those days the thickets were bigger and came closer to the
Sulphur. Only a little way south was Lake Caddo, and nobody
knew much about the lake but the Caddos and me.

We parted company at the Corners. "Better come with us,
Cull," Bob Lee advised. "You won't find anything but trouble
and knowing you like I think I do, you won't stand still for it."

"I'm a man wants to sleep under his own roof."

"You fight shy of that widow woman. She'll make you more
trouble than all them Union soldiers!" Longley said, grinning.

When they had dusted out of sight I turned that buckskin
mule down the grass-grown lane. This was a mighty good mule
and he could run the legs off most horses. Maybe he wasn't so
fast for a sprint but he could hold a pace that would kill most
horses, and better than any watchdog at night.

Longley mentioned a widow. With the war over this country
must be crowded with widows. Far as that went, this here was
a widow-making country, and leave out the war.

No decent woman would be wanting to have any truck with
me, and if one did it would surely come to a shooting matter
with a father or brother. Cullen Baker was a known man, a
trouble-hunter they used to say, and a man with a drive to kill,
others said. They said, too, I was drunken, but I could give
them the lie on that story. I'd little taste for strong drink, and
when they thought me drunk it was only with fury.

Besides, there'd be no time for widows. It would take all my
time to get a crop in, to work and even get my seed back; by
now the whole ranch might have grown up to crab grass.

Drawing my Dragoon Colt I checked the loads—paid a man

to be ready, although I was hoping never to use a gun again, except for wild game. Still, I've noticed a ready man is often left alone, and if it took that to have peace, then I should be ready, but it took no doing for me. I'd the habits of a lifetime behind me.

Right there in a secret pocket back of my belt there was the margin, a .41-caliber twin-barreled derringer which I carried for insurance. It was my margin of safety. Time was, a hide-out gun had been useful, and such a time might again come to me. Could be I'd never use either gun again, but I was no man to draw my teeth before I knew what the beef was like.

Turning the corner of the back lane along which I'd come, I drew up before the gate.

There it was, then.

Three years I'd waited to look upon it again, and the three years seemed like ten, or even fifteen. It seemed another lifetime, another world than this, and yet I was back. All was the same and yet nothing at all was the same.

The yard, which had been hard-packed earth there at the back of the house, had grown up to weeds and grass. The house itself looked older than it was, weather-beaten, blistered, baked and warped by sun and rain.

The sun, the rain, the wind let nothing alone, but they worry at it, smooth it and rough it again until it is their own. I was like that, myself. A man shaped by storms and hot suns, but most of all by the thousand storms I kept buried inside, all of them crowding at my lips and eyes for expression, working their way down into my quiet fingers, feeding anger through my veins that I'd had to fight back, again and again.

For what they said of me was true. I was a killing man, a man of frightful rages that all my life I'd had to keep back inside me. Once in a while when something would go against me, I'd tear loose and it frightened me, for I had no grudge against any man, nor did I know what it meant to hate. To be wary, yes, for I knew there were hating folks about, but for

13

myself, I hated no man. Only there was a point beyond which I'd not be pushed, and when beyond that point the fury came up in me, cold, dangerous and mighty.

Swinging down from the saddle I opened the gate, taking my time, almost scared to go in, for opening that gate was opening the memories I'd fought back for a long while now.

It seemed any minute Ma was going to open the door and call me for supper, or Pa would come, holding out his hand to greet me. Only they weren't going to come out, and nobody at all was coming to that door, which had remained unopened these two years now.

Leading the mule through the gate I dropped the bridle reins and walked slowly forward, and in my throat there was a lump.

Nobody was there. The kitchen door hung on old strap hinges, dried and shrunk from the neat fit Pa had given it when he built the place with his own hands, me helping as much as I could. A boy then I'd known little of the slights a man learns by working with his hands, and all I'd had to help was a strong back and arms for lifting.

The boards on the stoop were warped and gray, and brown leaves had gathered in the corner between the stoop and the house. Only the iris still grew along the path where Ma had planted it, and the redbud tree Pa and me dug up from the river's edge was well-grown now and making like a tree more than a shrub like they usually are. These things can last, I think, the trees a man plants and the wells he digs . . . I do not know if the buildings last.

The door opened stiffly under my hand, and when I went through the door there were tears down my cheeks like I was a pigtailed girl.

Empty, the way it was, it looked like I'd never seen it. Everything a body could carry off had been toted away except the big copper kettle near the fireplace which was unhandy to load on a horse. The rooms were empty and here and there the chunking had fallen from between the logs in the log part of the house which we had built first. Later, Pa started to build the rest of it with planks, and he was fixing to give Ma a real home at last. He never done it though, and hard work caught up with Ma first; she'd never been real strong.

She was buried out there back of the orchard, where they'd put Pa . . . somebody told me that; I'd not been here myself.

An owl had been roosting in the kitchen and left his sign around the way an owl does. A body would think there was fifty of them rather than one. There was dust over everything, and when Ma had lived there never was dust. She never had much to do with, but she made out, and that place had been spic and span like I'd never seen another place. It had been a home blessed by care if not by money.

At the fireplace I could see where night-stoppers had left the remains of their meal—only the mice had been at it.

Outside again, not liking the hollow sound of my feet on the board floors, I saw the weeds had grown up among the roses, and I could see there would be a sight of work to keep me busy.

"Well Pa," I said aloud, "what you wished it to be, that's what I'll make it."

When I went outside once more that old buckskin mule was cropping grass like it was the day before Judgment. Seeing he liked it so much, I picketed him there, and then took my Spencer and strolled down toward the swamp.

Ever go back to a place and walk down the paths you walked as a boy? The old paths, the unforgotten paths? The sun was hot on the green leaves and grass, the path was overgrown, and the blackberries had straggled over it and were choked with grass . . . many a time I snagged myself on those briars, and tore my shirt, too. The biggest, blackest and juiciest berries always seemed to hang in the places hardest to get at.

Every step was a memory for me, and time to time I'd just stop and stand there, remembering. The mist used to rise off

15

these swamps sometimes in the mornings. The tops of trees in the low ground would be like islands lost in a vast sea of cloud. Here was where the deer used to come to eat the green grass and get into Pa's corn—many a time I got me a deer down at the end of the cornfield.

It was warm and lazy in the sun and a big bumblebee buzzed fatly among the leaves. Folks are always talking about how busy a bee is, shows they never really watched a bee. A bee makes so much fuss with all his perambulating around that folks think they're doing a sight of work, but believe me, I've watched bees by the hour and I can tell you all that buzzing is a big fraud. The bees I've watched always buzzed in the sunniest places around the best-smelling flowers, just loafing their heads off fusting around in the play of sun and shadow at the swamp's edge. Busy? Not so's you could notice.

Used to be deer along the swamp edge but tonight my luck was played out, so I contented myself with a duck who got up lazy from the water, the dark, dark water among the lily pads. The Spencer took his head off just as he was clearing water so when I started back toward the place I had my supper. And then I heard voices and knew it was the sound of trouble.

Three mounted men at their horses in the yard, sizing up my mule. There was a tall man astride a mighty handsome bay gelding, and the next man was Joel Reese about whom I could remember nothing good, and the third man was a fellow with a face to remember—if a man was smart.

"Whose mule is that?" The man on the bay gelding was talking. There was authority in his voice, but my first impression was he was an empty man, impressed overmuch with himself, but knowing all the time there was nothing inside him. "You told me the place was deserted, Reese."

"Some rider-by or all-nighter," Reese explained. "The place has been abandoned for years and sometimes folks stop the night when passing through."

Looked to me like this was my time to talk up, for they had

16

not seen me yet. "The place isn't abandoned and it is not for sale," I said. "I'll be living here myself."

They turned sharp around to look at me, and Joel Reese grinned at me, with a mean glint in his little eyes. "Colonel, this is that Cullen Baker I told you about."

The colonel had a cold eye, and there was nothing pleasant in his eyes when he looked at me, but I'd looked into eyes over a gun barrel that were colder than these.

It was that third man who was holding my attention. The colonel was no fighting man and Reese would only fight if he had an edge, a big edge. But the other man was a different kettle of fish. That third man was a full-fledged red-in-the-comb fighting man who had grown his own spurs. I knew the type.

"Seems I should know you." I looked directly at him for the first time.

"The name is John Tower. I've come into the country since you left."

"Were you ever west of the Rockies?"

Tower's eyes became suddenly alive. "Could be," he said. "A man gets around."

The colonel interrupted. "Baker, you fought with the Confederacy. You are known hereabouts as a troublemaker. We will have no trouble from you, do you hear? The slightest evidence of trouble from you, or interference with the Reconstruction program, and you'll go to jail. Also, we're going to take steps to confiscate this land from you as an enemy of your country."

"You'd better look at your hole card, Colonel. There's no record of me fighting on any side. I've been out West the whole time. Only fighting I've done was with Comanches, Utes and such like."

"What's that?" The colonel turned on Reeves, his face growing red. The colonel was a man quick to anger. "Reese, is this true?"

17

Reese was worried. "Colonel Belser, sir, I just know he fit for the South! Why, why, there just ain't no other way he could fight!"

"Joel Reese," I explained, "was always a yellow dog. He should be right ashamed to mislead you this way. If he knows anything at all he should know that I spent the war in New Mexico and Utah. Shortly after the war broke out I drove a herd of cattle east and sold them, and then three years ago I went back West.

"Reese hates folks around here because they'd no use for him. My advice would be to go easy on anything he may tell you. He'd be like to cause you trouble, getting even with folks he figured treated him wrong."

"I need no suggestions from you!" Colonel Belser was furious. He jerked his bay around . . . no way to treat a horse as good as that one, or any other horse, for that matter. "The records will be checked as to your service with the Confederacy. You will hear from me again."

"I'll be right here," I told him. "I'll be growing corn."

Tower lingered as the others started off. "You were in New Mexico and Utah? And California?"

"I had a horse liked to travel."

"Have we crossed trails before this?"

"I cut a lot of sign in my time," I told him, "and once I've seen the tracks a man leaves, I don't forget."

"You mean that if you'd ever cut my trail you'd remember? Is that it?"

"I'd remember."

John Tower touched a spur to his mount and rode away after the others, and of them all he was the only one who might be dangerous in the way a man was dangerous. Yet he would come at a man, face up to him, and those others would not. It was not until they were out of sight that I turned and saw the girl under the dogwood tree.

It is a nice place to see a girl for the first time, and it had been a long, long time since I had seen such a girl. For girls of her type do not come to the Cullen Bakers of this world, for I was a rough man, grown used to rough ways, and I had no fine graces to use in meeting such a girl.

She was taller than most girls, with dark hair and a fair skin, and she stood very still with one uplifted hand upon a dogwood branch. She wore a white dress, and she was young, but there was in her eyes none of the guilelessness of the child. Beautiful, she was. Beautiful and graceful as the dogwood beside which she stood, a dogwood covered with white blossoms, some of them fallen to the grass at her feet.

"Did I surprise you?"

"You weren't expected, if that is what you mean."

"I am Katy Thorne, of Blackthorne."

There was no reason for me to love the Thornes, or even to think of them, for my only friend among them had been Will, and Will had been the strange one among the Thornes, whether those of Blackthorne or the others. His cousin Chance had been my worst enemy. And I remembered no Katy Thorne.

"You related to Chance?"

"I was his brother's wife."

"Was?"

"He tried to be a soldier and charged very gallantly with Pickett, at Gettysburg. Were you a soldier, Mr. Baker?"

"No." Maybe there was bitterness in the tone. "I have been nothing that mattered, Mrs. Thorne. I have never been anything but Cullen Baker."

"Isn't it important to be Cullen Baker?"

"Maybe, in the wrong way. Maybe"—why I said it I'll not know—"maybe I can make it mean something to be me. But hereabouts folks have little use for me, and I've less use for them."

"I know. I saw it begin, Cullen Baker, I was there at the mill the day you gave Chance Thorne a hiding."

"You were *there?*" I was astonished.

19

"Sitting in the surrey with my father and Will Thorne. I thought Chance deserved everything he got."

It was one day I'd not forget, for I'd come as a stranger with a sack of grain to the mill for grinding. We'd been down from Tennessee only a few days, and I'd not been off the place. Soon as I showed up Chance started on me, and the boys around followed his lead. He started making fun of my shabby home-spun clothes. They were patched and they were worn, but they were all I had. They had shouted at me and laughed at me but I'd taken my grain to the mill, and when I came out and started to hoist it to the mule's back they rushed at me and jerked my suspenders down and then they clodded me with chunks of dirt.

It wasn't in me to hurry. That was what made some of the men turn to watch, I think, for I heard somebody speak of it. The first thing I did, with clods splattering about me, was to pull up my pants and fix my suspenders. Then still with dirt splattering me, I hoisted my sack into place, and then I picked up a chunk of wood and started for them, and they scattered like geese, all but Chance Thorne.

He waited for me. He was a head taller than me, and some heavier, and he was dressed in store-bought clothes, which I'd never had and had only rarely seen. He looked at me and he was contemptuous. "Put down that club," Chance had said, "and I'll thrash you."

A dozen men were watching now, and none of them likely to be my friends. So when I put the club down he rushed me before I could straighten up, and he expected to smash my face with his fists as I tried to straighten, but in the Tennessee mountains a boy has to fight, and sometimes I'd fought men grown. So I didn't straighten, I just dove at his knees and brought Chance down with a thud.

He got up then, and I smashed his lips with my fist as he started to get up, like he'd tried with me, and my fist was hardened by work and it split his lips and covered his fine shirt with blood.

Maybe it was the first time Chance had seen his own blood and it shocked him, but it angered him, too. He walked at me, swinging both his fists, but there was a deeper anger in me, and an awful loneliness for there were boys cheering him on, and none of them with a shout for me. I was bitter lonely then, and it made the hate rise in me, and I walked into his fists driving with my own. There was nothing in him that could stand against the fierce anger I had, and he backed up, and there was a kind of white fear in his eyes. He sorely wanted help, he wanted to yell, but I ducked low and hit him in the belly, and saw the anguish in his face, and white to the lips I set myself and swung a wicked one square at that handsome face. He went down then and he rolled over in the dust, and he could have got up, but he didn't; he lay there in the dust and he was beaten, and I had an enemy for all my years.

Other men rushed from the mill then, Chance's father and uncle among them, and they rushed at me, so I backed to my club and picked it up. I was a lone boy but I was fierce angry with hating them and wanting to be away, and hating myself because I was afraid I would cry.

"Leave him alone!" I did not know Will Thorne then, a tall, scholarly man. "Chance began it."

Chance's father's face was flushed and angry. "You tend to your knitting, Will! I'll teach this young rascal to—"

He paused in his move toward me, for I'd backed to the mule and was set with my club. I was only a boy, but I was man tall and strong with work in field and forest. "You come at me," I said, "and I'll stretch you out."

He shook a fist at me. "I'll have you whipped, boy! I'll have you whipped within an inch of your life!"

Then I'd swing to my mule's back and rode away, but I did not ride fast.

And that was the beginning of it.

A few days later when I had come to town Thorne was waiting for me with a horse whip. When I'd started to dismount, he came at me with the whip, but seeing it coming I swung on the mule again and slammed him with my bare heels. Thorne was coming at me, but before he saw what was coming the mule was charging him. He drew back the whip too late, and the mule struck him with a shoulder and knocked him into the dust with half the town looking on. And then I had ridden out of town.

The next thing was worst of all, for the Thornes were good haters and they believed themselves the best in the community, with a reputation to uphold. We were working in the field, Pa and me, and four men came for me. Pa tried to stop them and one knocked him out with a club, and then they set on me with the whip. When they were through I was bloody and miserable, but not a sound did I make until they were gone. Then bloody and scarce able to walk, I helped Pa home and to bed, and put cold cloths on his head. Then I got down Pa's shotgun and started for town.

Haas and Gibson, two of the men who had done the whipping, were drinking their bonus in the saloon. When I got down from the mule it was past dark and the street was nigh empty. Up in front of the hotel I saw a man stop and look back, and then I'd stepped inside. Haas saw me first.

"Gib!" His voice was shaking. "Gib, *look!*"

Gibson turned and he reached for the pistol under his coat, and I shot, but not to kill. The shotgun was heavy loaded but I shot between them, close-standing as they were, and both men went down, both of them catching some shot.

They lay there shocked and bloody in the sawdust. "I done you no harm," I told them, "but you set on me an' Pa. Was I you I'd stay clear of us from now on, an' if Pa dies I'll kill the both of you."

Turning toward the door I stopped. "Don't you set up to give this boy no beating again, because I got the difference."

22

That was the summer I was fifteen.

Folks fought shy of me the few times I did come to town and I didn't come except when must be. Most of the year I spent in the swamps along the Sulphur, hunting, trapping, staying away from people, except the Caddos. But that had been the beginning of it. From then on I'd the reputation of a bad one and folks kept their daughters away from me, and even the men stayed clear of me.

Pa worked on, but he was never quite the same after that blow on the skull. Maybe it wasn't so much the blow what did the harm, but the feeling that here where he'd planned to start over, to build something of a place for Ma and me, here he had failed to do so. It was no fault of his, but he lost heart then and the fire went out of him. After Ma died he just continued on and went through the motions, but Pa was gone and I knew it.

Katy Thorne had reminded me and it all came back, the sound of Ma mixing batter in a wooden bowl, the weariness in Pa's face as he came up from the field, the morning singing of the birds, and the sullen splash of fish in the still water, the sound of dogs raising a coon out there on a still moonlit night.

These things had meant home to me, but Ma and Pa were gone and the memories of hunting wild cattle in the Big Thicket to the south was an empty memory, and the smell of damp earth and the warm sun of planting time . . . I had been a fool to come back.

"I've no cause to love the Thornes," I said, "only Will. I liked Will."

"I come here to gather flowers," she said. "I was surprised when I saw you."

Walking to the house I put my rifle down and started plucking the duck.

"You only fired once."

"There was only one duck."

She was silent, watching me as I worked. "A duck should hang for a while."

"He'll do his hanging inside me then. This is my supper."

"It's a small supper for a hungry man. Come to Blackthorne for supper. There's a baked ham."

"Do you know what you're asking, ma'am? Cullen Baker to come to Blackthorne? I could not do it without a shooting, and even if that was avoided people would speak no more to you. I've a black name along the Sulphur."

"You've been gone a long time, Cullen Baker. Blackthorne is deserted now, and has been since the war ended. It is Will's house that I live in, and which he left to me when he died. Aunt Flo is with me there, and you're not likely to see anyone but her."

"Chance?"

"He's in Boston, or wherever, and he does not often come to call, anyway. Chance likes the towns of Texas, not the plantations and ranches."

It would not be the first time I had been to the house of Will Thorne, for even as I made enemies that day at the mill, I had also made a friend.

Will Thorne, in my estimation, was a man worth the lot of them, perhaps less the sportsman than the others, and much less the talker, but a man of some attainments in his own way. He studied nature a good bit, and I who had lived in the swamps found much to learn from him, as he, I suppose, learned from me.

He did a sort of writing. I never knew much about that as I was a man who had learned to read but poorly, scarcely more than my name, which I could write, and no more. But he wrote some things for periodicals in London and in Paris, one was about a heron we have in the swamps, and another was on the beaver. I believe he wrote about butterflies and trap-door spiders, and a variety of things. It made no sense to me at first; I'd known about those things from a child, and he told me once that I'd knowledge in my head a naturalist would give years of his life to own.

We had walked in the swamps. The trails were known to none but the Caddos and me, though later I showed a few of them to Will, and sometimes we'd hunt for plants together, or for strange birds or insects. Usually I knew where to find what he wanted, for a man who is much in the woods acquires a gift for observation.

In Will I had a friend, and I never forgot his one question after I'd told him of some fight—there were others after the one at the mill, like the one at Fort Belknap when I killed a man—all he would say was to ask me, "Do you think you did the right thing?"

A question like that sticks in a man's mind, and after awhile I judged everything by it, deciding whether it was the right thing, and often if there was no other way. I expect it was a good lesson to learn, but a man in his life may have many teachers, some most unexpected. The question lies with the man himself: Will he learn from them?

For a man to be at peace with himself was important, Will said, not what people say. People are often wrong, and public opinion can change, and the hatreds of people are rarely reasonable things. I can hear him yet. He used to say there was no use a man wearing himself out with hatred and ill-feeling, and time proved it out.

"Will used to tell me about you when I was a little girl," Katy said. "He said you were a fine boy. That you'd the makings of a fine man if they would just let you alone. But he said you'd the makings of a great clansman in the old days among the Highlands of Scotland. He said you'd dark blood in you, dangerous blood. But he always came back to saying you were the best of them around here, thoughtful, he used to say, and a gentleman at heart."

Despite myself, I was embarrassed at that. It has been rare that anyone has given me a word of praise in my life, and the last thing I'd thought of myself was a good man. But it worried me some, for Will Thorne was a man of few mistakes, and his

25

saying that put a burden on me, his saying I was a good man almost put it up to me to be one. The idea was uncomfortable, for I'd been busy being Cullen Baker, and what he'd said about the black angers I could grasp, for it was proved too often in my life.

We sat in the kitchen to talk, and I liked the rustle of her skirts as she moved about, making friendly sounds with glass and crockery, and tinkling a bit of silver now and again. The fire made a good homely sound, too, and the water boiling in the pot. I was a man unused to such sounds, knowing the crackling of a fire from my own lonely camps and not from a hearth.

Aunt Flo was napping somewhere in the house while Katy got supper, and it was a rare surprise to me to see how sure she was about it, with no finagling and nonsense, but with deft hands and of one mind about what to do. I'd never thought to see a Thorne preparing her own meal, least of all a meal for me.

She put the dishes on a small table in a corner of a room, a friendly sort of table, and not like the long one in the dining room, which scared me to look at, it was so far from end to end. There she lighted the candles, and a soft glow they made, which was as well, for I'd had no chance to shave the day, and my clothes were shabby and worn from riding in all kinds of weather. I was shy about them, the big hulking fool that I was, and no man to be eating supper with such a girl.

Yet she was easy to be with, easier than any girl I'd met, and here and there I'd known a few, although not always of the nicest. The sort you tumble in the hay with, or take a walk with out in the grass away from the wagons. Yes, I'd known them, but some of them were good girls, too. Maybe it was wrong of me to walk out with them that way, but when the urge is on a man his conscience is often forgot.

"Tell me about the West," Katy asked me over coffee. "It

has always fascinated me. If I had been a man, I should have gone West."

Tell her of the West? Where could a man begin? Where could he find words to put the pictures before her that he saw when she asked about the West? How could he tell her of fifty-mile drives without water and the cattle dying and looking wild-eyed into the sun? How could he tell her about the sweat, the dust, the alkali? Or the hard camps of hard men where a word was ·a gun and a gun was a death? And plugging the wound with a dirty handkerchief and hoping it didn't poison? What could a man tell a woman of the West? How could he find words for the swift-running streams, chuckling over rocks, for the mountains that reached to heaven and the clouds that choked the valleys among the high peaks? What words did he have to talk of that?

"There's a wonder of land out there, Mrs. Thorne," I said, "a wide wonder of it, with distances that reached out beyond your seeing where a man can ride six days and get nowhere at all. There are canyons where no white man has walked, canyons among the unfleshed bones of the mountains, with the soil long gone if ever there was any, like old buffalo bones where the buzzards and coyotes had been at them. There's campfires, ma'am, where you sit over a tiny fire with a million tiny fires in the sky above you like the fires of a million lonely men. You hover over your fire and hear the coyotes speaking their plaintive words at the moon, and you smell the acrid smoke and you wonder where you are and if there's Comanches out there, and your horse comes close to the fire for company and looks out into the dark with pricked-up ears. Chances are the night is empty, of living things, anyway, for who can say what ghosts may haunt a country the like of that?

"Sometimes I'd be lazy in the morning and lie in my blankets after sunup, and I'd see deer coming down to the waterhole to drink. Those days a man didn't often camp right up against a waterhole. It wasn't safe, but that wasn't the reason. There's

27

other creatures need water besides a man, and they won't come nigh it if a man is close by, so it's best to get your water and then sleep back so the deer, the quail, and maybe a cougar can come for water, too.

"Times like that a man sees some strange sights. One morning I watched seven bighorn sheep come down to the water. No creature alive, man or animal, has the stately dignity of a bighorn. They came down to water there and stood around, taking another drink now and again. Tall as a burro most of them, and hair as soft as a fawn's belly. A man who travels alone misses a lot, ma'am, but he sees a lot the busy, talky folks never get a chance to see.

"Why, I've stood ten feet from a grizzly bear stuffing himself with blackberries and all he did was look at me now and again. He was so busy at those berries he'd no time for me. So I just sat down and watched him and ate my own fixin's right there, for company. He paid me no mind, and I paid him little more. When I'd eaten what I had, I went back to my horse and when I left I called out to him and said, 'Goodbye, Old Timer,' and lifted a hand, and would you believe it, ma'am, he turned and looked after me like he missed my company."

I was silent, suddenly embarrassed at having talked so all-fired much. It wasn't like me to go to talking like that. Shows what candlelight and a pretty woman can do to a man's judgment of the fitness of things.

Aunt Flo had not come down, although I heard some stirring about upstairs. For me it was just as well. I'm no hand at getting acquainted with people in bunches. I'd rather cut one out of the herd and get acquainted slow-like so I can really know what the person is like. Never much of a talker I'd little business with women. It's been my observation that the men with fluent tongues are the ones who get the womenfolks, and a slick tongue will get them even faster than money.

"If you loved it so much out there, Cullen, why did you come back?"

Well . . . there was that question I'd been asking myself, and of which I didn't rightly know the answer. There were answers I'd given myself, however.

"It's all the home I ever had," I told her, trying to make the words answer my own problem. "My folks are buried out there back of the orchard where Ma used to walk. The land is mine, and it is good land. Pa would work from daylight to dark out there, trying to make it pay. I don't know, maybe it was a feeling I had for him or just wanting to be some place familiar, and there was nothing out West that belonged to me. Maybe, rightly speaking, I'm no wanderer at all, but just a homebody who would rather be unhappy among familiar surroundings and faces than happy anywhere else."

"I don't believe that." Katy got up to clear the dishes. "And don't call me Mrs. Thorne. We're old friends, Cullen. You must call me Katy."

Standing up I seemed most too high for the little room where we'd been eating, so I fetched dishes to the kitchen and got my hat to go.

"Come again, Cullen, when you've a wish to talk or want a meal cooked by other than your own hands."

At the door I paused. "Katy . . . ma'am, the light must be out when I go out the door. There's folks about would just as soon have a shot at me if the chance was there."

Outside in the dark I stepped to the side of the door and let my shadow lose itself in the shadow of the house. Caution becomes a man in strange country, and this country would be strange to me for a few days until the feel was in me again.

At night all places have a feeling of their own, and a man must be in tune with the night if he is to move safely. The sounds were different, and a man's subconscious has to get used to them again, so standing there against the outer wall of Will's house, I listened into the night, my mind far ranging out over the great lawns of Blackthorne, which were off to my left, and the orchard to my right, and beyond that to the swamps the river was bringing closer to Blackthorne by the year.

The frogs were loud in the darkness, a cricket chirped nearby. No coyote sounds in here, although there were wolves enough in the thickets to the south and west. Somewhere an owl hooted, and something splashed out in the swamp. The night was quiet so I walked to where the mule had been left and tightened the girth, then adjusted the bridle. It was quiet enough, but the mule was alert and I was uneasy.

Maybe it was the strangeness after so many desert and prairie nights, but turning from the path to the lane, I took a way that led back through the orchard and so across the fields. It made no kind of practical sense, going back the way I'd come—a man in Indian country learns things like that because it is back along the return trail they may be waiting for you.

The night had a different smell, a familiar smell. The clean dryness of the desert air, touched by the smell of sage or cedar was gone. Here there was a heaviness of the greater humidity, and heavier smells of decaying vegetation, of stagnant water, and of dew-wet grass. The leaves of the peach trees brushed my hat as I rode through the orchard, taking my way from old experience toward a place where the fence was down. Sure enough, it had never been fixed.

When I walked the mule across the soft grass coming up back of my own house I knew there was someone else around, and drew up, careful not to shift my weight so the saddle would creak, and then I listened. Then an owl hooted and I had a feeling it was no true owl but one speaking for me.

Searching a minute in my mind I tried to recall what Bob Lee knew of our place and where, if it was him, he would wait, and was sure and certain it would not be the house itself.

There was a big old stump Pa had never been able to grub out, gigantic roots, big as small trees themselves, curled deep into the rich earth and without powder, which we could not afford then, it would be a long task to get it out. So we left it there, and it was a known place, used for a meeting on coonhunting nights. Bob Lee would remember. One of the few times he'd been on the place was to coon hunt, so I swung in a wide circle toward the stump, and when I was backed by the trees I hooted like an owl, but low down, so I'd sound farther off than I was . . . in the night a knowing man can do many things with sound.

The answer was plain, so with the Spencer in shooting position I walked that mule over the weed-grown field toward the stump. Two men arose from its shadow as I pulled up.

"Cullen?" it was Bob Lee.

"You've the name. What's the message?"

"Chance Thorne has learned you're here. He's sworn to drive you from the country. You were seen by someone in the lanes today, and then you've talked to Joel Reese."

"If he comes for me, he'll find me here. I've work to do."

"If the time comes you've a need of friends," Bob Lee said, "you'll know where to find us. We've means of learning things, Cullen, and friends about who'll feed us and hide us as well."

Crouched by that big old stump we talked an hour away, and they brought me up to date on much that had taken place, and things they'd just got wind of. Bob Lee was a man with friends as well as a big family, and such can be a sight of comfort to a man, times like this.

Bill Longley had little to say. He was stern for his age, a tall, quiet young man that took getting used to, but I liked him.

"You know what I think," Bob Lee said, standing. "I think we'll all be lucky if we add five years to our ages. I think they've marked us down for dying."

"Five years?" Longley's tone was almost wistful. "Bob, I'd settle for the certain knowledge of one year."

Bob Lee stood silent, a fine man, but with sharp-honed pride brought to an edge by family position and the anger in him that he had to run, I'd have said he would be lucky to last the year. As for me, I intended to fight shy of trouble. The

31

carpetbaggers would pass as all things do, and I'd show my patience—although I'd little of that—and try to wait them out.

"We'll have small chance," Bob Lee said, "unless we're armed and ready. You'd better give thought to that, Cullen, and go to your plow with your Spencer in a scabbard on the plow handle."

"This land is mine," I said. "I mean to crop it, and I'll buy cattle when I can, and horses, too. I mean to breed horses here, when it can be safely done."

"There's wild cattle in the thickets, Cullen. We could get together and round up a bunch and drive them to Fort Worth. If you want, tell me and I can have fifty men for you in a couple of days."

"There's that many?"

"In the thickets? There's more, man. And they'll fight, if it comes to that."

"I want no fighting. It is peace I have come for, and it is peace I will have."

When they were gone I waited until the sound of their going had faded away, losing itself among the night sounds. What Bob Lee had said was true. If they came upon me in the fields it would be well to have a gun, for it was always better to talk peace with a solid argument at hand. The Spencer carbine was not too long, easy to swing into line, but I must have another Colt. It was a hard-hitting pistol with a good range.

Yet it was not of peace I was thinking when the trouble came. It was of Katy Thorne.

There was a faint whisper of a boot in the grass but my mind was elsewhere and the warning was an instant late. A gun jammed hard against my spine and a hand wrenched the Colt from my belt and another hand, rising almost from the ground, grasped the barrel of my Spencer. The gun muzzle at my back was an insistent argument, I relaxed my hold on the carbine and stood quiet.

"Welcome home, Cullen." That would be the voice of Chance

Thorne, and a fine voice he had, faintly mocking now. "I was afraid you had gone for good."

At the moment there was nothing to say, and certainly nothing to do. Lee and Longley would be deep into the swamp by now, and whatever was done I must do myself. So I stood very still and I think my silence began to worry them.

"Shall we take him back?" It was Reese speaking. "Or just leave him here?"

"The colonel wishes to speak to him, but the colonel is sure he will resist, so naturally he expects to see him in rather rough condition, and in a mood to answer questions."

Reese said, "What are we waiting for?" And struck out viciously. And as he struck I kicked him in the groin. He screamed out like an animal in pain, and then they closed in around me. My swinging fist smashed at a face and I had the savage pleasure of feeling the bone crunch, and then I plunged forward, punching with both hands, fighting to get clear of the circle. And then out of nowhere a pistol barrel caught me across the skull and my knees went rubbery and I fell, and then they closed in, kicking and striking as I rolled on the ground, trying to evade them. Their very numbers interfered with brutality.

Suddenly Chance parted the group and said, "I waited a long time for this!" And he kicked me in the head.

Only a quick turn of my head saved me the full force of that kick, but I pushed my face into the soft grass and relaxed as if unconscious, which I nearly was. There was a heavy throbbing inside my skull and I wondered if it had been cracked, and vaguely I heard someone say, "Throw him over a horse." And in the brief moment before consciousness slipped away, I felt a swift, savage exultation that so far they had not found my derringer.

Only I knew that I must live. Regardless of everything, I must live and make them pay. They had come upon me in a mob, too cowardly to face me alone, and no man deserves to be beaten and hammered by a mob, and the men who make up a mob are cowards. But cowards can die, and being cowards death is a bitterness beyond anything a brave man can feel.

"You take my advice," I heard Joel Reese say, "and you'll hang him now."

"Did I ask your advice?" Chance spoke contemptuously. "Did I ever take your advice?"

When they threw me over the horse I was only vaguely conscious, but when the horses started down the lane I knew I had a chance if they kept on along this route. It was a slim chance, but I'd no intention of taking any more than I'd had; as long as they believed me unconscious I had a chance.

The rider who rode the horse over which they'd thrown me had kicked me in the head when mounting, and the boot in the stirrup was beside my skull, and I could hear the slight tinkle of the spur. When they made the turn along the swamp it was my chance and it had to come now. Grabbing the boot I jammed the spur into the horse's ribs as hard as I could shove.

It was unexpected, the man's foot was easy in the stirrup, and the startled horse lunged in pain, plunging off the trail into the brush and grass, and when the horse plunged I went off the saddle into the edge of the swamp.

There was a mad moment while the rider fought his horse before he was aware of what had happened, and in that moment I reached my feet and made three fast strides, and then dove head-first into the brush, squirming forward. Behind me there were shouts, screams of fury, and then shots cut the brush past my head. The earth turned to mud and then water and I splashed through the reeds and rank water-grass and lowered myself into the dark water.

There was an instant when my hand slid along a mossy log and I shuddered, thinking it an alligator, and then I half-waded, half-swam over to a mud bank and crawling out, lay gasping with pain.

My skull pounded like a huge drum, every throb was one of

pure agony, and my body was wracked with pain, bruised from the kicking, and bloody as well. And that blood would mean added danger in the swamp.

Yet I knew my position would be secure only for minutes, and after that, I had to move.

Behind me there were shouts and the splashing and cursing of the searchers.

This was my first night at home, and already I was a hunted man. Deep within me there was a pounding hatred of those who had done this to me. They had mobbed me, beaten me, and for no reason. Yet *they* had declared war, *I* had not. Be it on their own heads, I told myself. Whatever comes now, they have asked for it.

TWO

After a time my breath came easier, and I lay very still, trying to plan. I had come no more than sixty feet from that swampy shore, and I knew this bank upon which I lay sprawled for I had fished from it many a time. It was only a narrow, projecting tongue of swampy ground that reached out like a pointing finger into the dark waters.

It was this vicinity that was favored by the huge old 'gator locally known as Ol' Joe, and reputed to have eaten more than three men, yet it was this water I must swim, and there was no other way out. It could be no more than a minute or two before either Chance Thorne or Joel Reese remembered the mud bar.

To walk back to the mainland was to invite capture, for already the search along the shore was nearing the connecting point. Getting to my feet I hobbled across the mud bar to the far side.

There was a knifing pain in my side, and one leg was badly bruised and probably torn. Ol' Joe was a chance I had to accept, wherever he was he would be sure to catch the scent of blood in the water. On the other hand it would make the pursuers no more eager to investigate until daylight.

Walking into the dark water until it was chest-high, I struck out. Swimming was something at which I'd always been handy, and I moved off into the water making almost no sound. Despite the throbbing in my skull and the stiff, bruised muscles I must swim about two hundred yards into the swamp before there would be a place to land.

Taking each stroke by itself, neither thinking nor trying to plan beyond the other side, I swam steadily, keeping my mind away from Ol' Joe.

Behind me there was a shout of triumph and I knew they had found some tracks. Glancing back I saw lanterns bobbing along the swamp shore.

Somewhere out here, and my swimming should have put me in a direct line with them, were a few old cypresses standing in the water. They were heavy with Spanish moss and a tangle of old boughs and might offer a hide-out. A few minutes later my hand struck an underwater root, then feeling around, caught a low-hanging limb. Taking a good grip I pulled myself up out of the water.

The air was cold after the water and my teeth chattered. From limb to limb I climbed until there was a place on some twisted limbs where I could make a nest for myself. Removing my belt I belted myself around a branch of the tree and lay there in the darkness, teeth rattling with cold, mosquitoes swarming around.

The last thing I recalled was the lights along the shore line and then I must have slept or become unconscious for when I opened my eyes again the sky was gray in the east, and their campfires were large on the shore, waiting for daylight and serious search.

Something was wrong with one of my eyes and when I felt of it with careful fingers I found it swollen enormously, and fast shut. There was a great welt above one ear, and a wide cut on my scalp. Every muscle was stiff and sore, and my head throbbed with a dull pound. The flesh of my left arm was badly torn by the hobnails of a boot, and only the fact that it had been cushioned from beneath by grass and soft earth had saved it from breaking. No matter how I felt, I could wait no longer, for this place while good enough at night, would never survive a search by day.

Peering about, turning my head awkwardly because of the one eye I could use, I searched for some escape. And then I glimpsed a huge old log half concealed by vines. It was afloat, but hung up on a root of the very cypress where I was hiding.

There was movement around the fires and their voices carried to me as I climbed down the tree, every move painful, and my head feeling like a keg half-full of water, sloshing around and hard to manage.

By bending branches I got the log loose. By the sound of the voices I knew the searchers were drinking, which would make it worse for me if caught. Then pushing the log free with a broken branch for a pole, I started to move. The swamp was one of the arms of Lake Caddo, which nobody knew much about, and my guess was that a hundred years from now, folks still would not know all its tortuous sloughs and the hyacinth-clogged bayous of sluggish brown water. Yet around this lake with its bayous and sloughs, and the swamps along the Sulphur I'd spent most of my boyhood, and I figured to know this swamp country in both Louisiana and Texas as well as anybody.

Keeping that clump of cypress between the shore and me, I poled steadily, every bruised muscle aching, pushing deeper and deeper into the swamp. Where I was going now they would not follow me even if they knew of it, and I was mighty sure they didn't. I was going to the island.

No more than a half-dozen men knew of that island before the war, and probably nobody had learned of it since unless taken there by one of those who knew. Hidden from sight in a wilderness of moss-hung cypress, the approaches seemingly clogged by hyacinth or lily pads, the island was a quarter of a mile long, and at its widest no more than a hundred yards. The highest point was about six feet above the water, but without a guide who knew the area the island simply could not be found. From a dozen yards away it was invisible in the jungle of trees, moss and vines. The Caddo Indians had known of it, and a few of the mixed-blood Caddo-Negroes who lived in the swamp knew of it.

There were several of these islands, although the others were smaller and, but for one other, more exposed. Yet it was likely that none of them were known to these fellows who mostly had ridden down from Boston, Texas.

A heron flew up and spread wide wings . . . poling on along the bayou, my head throbbing, muscles aching, finding a way through the lilies that would close after me.

How far had I come? A mile? Two miles? Moving as though in a trance, thinking only of putting distance between myself and the searchers who must now be looking for me. If they caught up with me before I reached the island I would be caught with nothing but the derringer to protect me, and it was useless at a distance. Moreover, I needed rest and a chance to gather my strength after the brutal beating I'd taken. My only chance was on that island where I was almighty sure Bob Lee, Longley and maybe Bickerstaff would be.

The sun was hot, and the water dead and still. Occasionally there were wide pools to cross, but mostly it was a matter of finding a way through the fields of lilies and hyacinth that choked many wide areas. If Ol' Joe had been around he certainly wasn't making himself known to me.

Every move of the pole was an effort now. Sometimes I could touch no bottom for some distance, nor could I always pole off the hyacinth although in most places there was enough thick growth to give a man some purchase. When I reached those places where I touched no bottom I just had to float, or paddle a bit with my hands to keep moving.

The sun was terribly hot and I needed water. The swamp water could be drunk if a man needed it bad enough, but folks got fever from it, I'd heard, and I was in trouble enough.

And I was still poling along, half-delirious when the log run aground. Several times I tried to force it on, and then looked up through a haze of pain and saw the bank of the island rising before me. But it was not a part of it that I remembered. Clumsily, I scrambled up the bank and fell flat, lying in the warm sunshine, letting the tired muscles relax. My brain was foggy and I seemed to have a hard time getting to my feet, but I knew that I must keep moving. The swamp has a way of destroying anything that becomes helpless, and to keep moving was my only salvation.

The earth was damp and in deep shadow once I left the shore, except where here and there the foliage overhead thinned out allowing enough sunlight to dapple the earth with light and shadow. Once, so weak that if it had been closer I could not have avoided it, I passed a huge diamond-back rattler coiled on a log.

Once, staggering, I fell to my knees and doubted whether I could get up—somehow I did. Vaguely then, my surroundings grew familiar. So on I went, although my strength seemed gone. Stumbling, falling, often entangled in brush, twice wading almost neck-deep in water, I kept going until struggling through the last forest of cattails I crawled up on a grassy shore near the camp. And there Bill Longley found me.

There were three days then of which I remember nothing. Then, slowly, the cuts and abrasions healed, and my head stopped its throbbing. The fierce anger faded, but left behind a sullen hatred. And there was desperation also, for it seemed a door was closing behind me, and that whatever I had come back for was slipping away, and would be lost.

Loafing about the island camp, I tried to think things out. This must not stop me. True it was that I had been set upon and beaten, yet if ever I was to be anything but what I was, I

41

must make myself a man of substance, of property. And my only chance for that was to return to the land, to plant my crops, to buy my stallion and brood mares, and to win the fight on my own terms.

My immediate reaction was to get a gun and hunt them down, one by one, saving Chance for the last, and kill each man of them who had set upon me.

Yet there had been enough of killing, and, at the end, where would I be? An outlaw and a hunted man, without friends, without a place in the world. It would be too easy to be whipped, to sit back and admit that I'd been defeated. Down inside I knew they'd made me eat dirt, but it had been the dirt of my own field, and I could find it not unappetizing.

There were a dozen men on the island now. Bob Lee was there, so was Bill Longley and Bickerstaff, who was a good man and a hard one. All of these men were only a generation removed from those who fought at the Alamo and San Jacinto.

Listening to their desultory conversation I kept to my own thoughts with half my mind. There was that land Pa owned down on Big Cypress Bayou, the place called Fairlea. It was situated in an out-of-the-way place, surrounded on three sides by swamp and forest. On the west there was, as I recalled, a narrow grass-grown lane along the property line. It was fenced off, concealed, yet good land and a part of a place Pa had bought for a pittance. I strongly doubted whether anyone in either Boston or Jefferson dreamed it was owned by Pa. Fairlea was my best chance.

Bob Lee disagreed. "You've too many enemies. You'll not get a chance to get your crop in, to say nothing of harvesting."

"It's my feeling," I told them. "Nobody authorized my arrest. I've a thought it was Chance Thorne, acting on his own. There's still a chance they'll leave me alone."

"Maybe," Longley said dryly. "But there's some who will remember you and be afraid, and men try to destroy anybody they are scared of."

"There's something else we've got to talk about," Bickerstaff suggested, "and that's Barlow. We're getting blamed for every thieving, murdering thing he does while he hides out in the Thickets."

"He has friends tipping him off," Jack English declared. "He always knows where the Army isn't goin' to be."

While they talked of that my mind wandered back to that lonely field at Fairlea. With luck a man could get a crop into the ground there and nobody the wiser. Then with some feed to stash away I might even go wild-cow hunting down in the Thickets and come out with a herd we could drive to Sedalia or Montgomery.

Of this much I was almighty sure: they'd not take me again and treat me as they had just now. I'd see them all in hell first, and go with them if need be. And that brought back the problem of defense. Nothing could be done until I had a gun, until I had a carbine and a Dragoon Colt.

So I got to my feet and started toward my mule which Bill Longley had brought to the island for me. Jack English had gone with him to get it, and for that I owed them a debt that I must pay.

Lee watched me saddle up the mule. "You fixin' to go somewhere, Cull?"

"Figure I'll need my guns. I'm goin' after them."

Longley had been lying on the ground chewing a blade of grass. Now he sat up and regarded me curiously, but he let the others do the talking.

"You figure to do it alone?" Lee asked mildly.

"A man forks his own broncs in this country," I told him, "but I've nothing against you riding along if you've a might to."

"Well, now," Longley got to his feet, "I sort of figure this might be somethin' to see."

Four of them rode along: Bob Lee, Jack English, Bickerstaff and Longley. I'd have wanted no better men, anywhere.

Jefferson lay lazy in the afternoon sun. A child rolled a hoop along the boardwalk, and a dog lay sprawled in the dust in the center of the street, flopping his tail as they rode by to indicate his satisfaction with things as they were and a willingness to let things be. Two men dozed against the wall of a store enjoying the shade and their chronic idleness.

The street was silent. A few men riding into the street meant nothing to anybody, not those days. There were loose men from everywhere, just drifting, hunting they knew not what, men who had lost what they had in the war and were hoping, away back inside their skulls, to find it somewhere else.

It wasn't likely any of them would know me on sight, although, come to think of it, Joel Reese had. But then I was on the place and where a body might expect me to be.

Stepping down from my mule, I glimpsed my reflection in the store window, a strapping big man in a cabin-spun shirt that was a size too small; my shoulders packed a lot of heavy muscle in them and it swelled that shirt considerable. First money I came by would have to go into clothes or I'd be seedplanting naked as a jaybird.

The black hair curled over the back of my shirt collar, and I guess I looked like an uncurried broomtail, one of those wild ponies folks find running in the swamps or the off-shore islands.

We had pulled up in front of the military headquarters, and I walked right in, asking nobody yes or no. There was a soldier dozing on a chair near the door with a rifle across his knees. He gaped at me, then started to pick up that rifle but something in my eyes made him change his mind. Maybe it was because I was a-figuring to stretch him out if he made a move to swing that gun on me. And I was positioned to do it.

This soldier was the Reconstruction vintage, if you know what I mean. He was no veteran. Likely he never killed nothing more than a squirrel, or something he could aim at two hundred yards off . . . It was a sight different to look up and see a full-grown man staring at him, just a-waiting for him. This

boy had a uniform coat and cap, but only homespun pants—
and he was asking for no trouble.

Colonel Amon Belser was there. He was tipped back in his
chair looking at some papers and when he looked over them he
saw me. I don't think he liked what he saw.

"Colonel," I said, "Chance Thorne came out to my place the
other night and set on me. The men with him took my pistol
and my Spencer, and gave me a sight of a whipping to boot. I
came to get my guns back."

This Belser was surprised, but he was no fool. He sat very
still, trying to think it out before he spoke. I had an idea
Chance had operated on his own, but Chance was not a good
man to cross and, unless I missed my guess, Chance was a
man who would have influence.

"If you received a beating," Belser said stiffly, "no doubt you
deserved it. I know nothing about your guns."

"This here country," I said, "a man needs a gun. Lots of
mighty mean folks riding the roads these nights. I'd like my
guns, Colonel."

Belser was angry. He was top man here and not used to
being talked to like that. "Baker," he said to me, "you get out
of here! And get out of town! I know nothing about your guns,
but from what I've heard of you, you're better off without
them."

Well, sir, right then I leaned over the desk and picked up
the brand-new, spanking-new Dragoon Colt that lay there on
the desk. Then I spun the cylinder and checked the action. It
was in working shape and fully loaded.

"Then I'll just have to take this one," I told him, speaking
mildly. "And it looks like a fine weapon."

"Put that down!" Belser could get authority in his voice
when he was a might to. "That's my pistol!"

Well, now. Putting that pistol behind my waistband I shoved
open the little gate in the fence that kept folks back from him,
and walked over to the rifle rack. There were several guns

there, but one of them was a Spencer carbine, a sight newer
and much finer than the one I'd had taken off me. It was
loaded too.

Belser got up suddenly and started for me and I just turned
around. Holding the carbine belt-high thataway it was just
almost naturally pointed at his belt buckle. Lead taken on a full
stomach is mostly just indigestible, middle of the day, especially.

Belser stopped. He didn't want to stop, I could see that, but
maybe he was having trouble with his digestion and didn't
want anything to upset his stomach. Man like that, he has
worries, and it doesn't pay to take anything on your stomach
you can't rightly handle. He was mad with himself for stopping, but he stopped.

"Colonel," I told him, and I spoke quiet-like. "I came back
to the Sulphur River country to mind my own affairs. When I
came back here I wanted no trouble with any man, but I've
been set on and beaten. Now I know the men who did it, and
when I figure the time is right, I'll talk to each and every one
of them. I'll read them from the Scriptures, Colonel, but in my
own good time.

"Seems to me you'd want it quiet here. Seems folks back
Washington way and down about Austin, seems like they might
figure you weren't handling things right if a lot of trouble was
stirred up down here. Now you leave me alone and you tell
Chance Thorne to lay off me, and I'll make no trouble for you.
You start something against me, Colonel, and I'll run you the
hell out of the country."

That soldier, he sat right still, keeping his eyes on the floor,
and wanting no trouble. So I just kept the guns I'd taken, and I
walked right out of there into the street.

That tall, lean, long-headed Longley was leaning against an
awning post right across the street, smoking a black cigar. Bob
Lee was standing by the hitch rail on my own side of the
street, looking mighty accidental-like. At the end of the street

Jack English was squatting on his heels playing mumblety-peg with his bowie knife.

"Long as we're here," Longley said, "I figure we should have us a drink."

English, he stayed where he was, keeping an eye out for trouble, but the rest of us started for the saloon. Just about that time the saloon door opened and Joel Reese walked out.

He started to stretch and he caught himself right in the middle of it, and he stood there staring at me like his spine had come unsnapped, his face turning kind of sick gray.

"Bob," I said, "this gent is one of those who entertained me the other night. Fact is, he was one of those calling the numbers for the dance. I figure this man should be instructed in the Word of the Lord."

"Yes, sir," Bob Lee was mighty serious, "you take your text from Job, fourth chapter, eighth verse: 'They that plow iniquity and sow wickedness, they shall reap the same.' "

Joel Reese took a sort of half-step back, looking around for help. Longley had moved around to cut him off and he was standing there, lazy-like, his thumbs hooked in his belt, but boy though he was, there was nothing soft about Bill Longley.

Reese, he looked at me and he set up to say something but I wasn't figuring on much talk. So I slapped him across the mouth. Well, sir, I'm a big man and I have done a sight of work in my time, and I was remembering how they had closed in on me the other night, so that slap shook him up, somewhat.

He struck out at me, and I just shifted my feet to make the blow miss and slapped him again. That time it started blood from his nose.

Colonel Belser came to the door and he had a rifle in his hands. "Here! Stop that!"

Now Bill Longley had him a Dragoon Colt in his hand and he was looking right at the colonel. "Mister Belser, sir," he said that, only he dragged it out a might, "you see a sinner being shown that the way of the transgressor is hard, and

47

Colonel, sir, should you transgress any further with that weepon, you will transgress yourself right into a belly full of lead."

To bring his rifle to bear Colonel Belser must turn a quarter of the way around, and you could see with half an eye that he realized it. Bill Longley was standing there holding that pistol sort of casual-like, and down there at the end of the street, not too far off, was Jack English, just a-setting there. The good colonel must have had it brought home to him that there was no way he could turn without turning right into a chunk of lead. Right then I'd bet he was some unhappy with himself for not staying right inside and giving an imitation of a man gone deaf, dumb and blind.

While Belser stood there unwilling to chance a move, I remembered very clearly what had happened to me in my own yard, so I slapped Reese into a first-class beating. "Next time," I told the colonel, "it will be a shooting matter."

Now I didn't know this at the time, but in his office overlooking the street Judge Tom Blaine was watching all that took place, but the judge was no carpetbagger. Judge Tom had fought in the Mexican War, and it had hurt him to see Jefferson folks afraid of these ragtag soldiers of the Reconstruction.

There were things we needed, so while the others mounted up and held my mule for me, I walked down the street to buy ammunition. It was just as I was finishing buying what I needed that Katy Thorne came into the store, and when she saw my face, I saw her own eyes go wide with surprise and hurt.

My face was still bruised and the cuts had only half-healed, and I suspect I was a sight to see. "Chance told me what they had done," she said, "but I didn't believe it was so bad."

"I'll have a talk with Chance."

She caught my sleeve. "Cullen, why don't you go away? They'll not leave you alone, you must know that! Even if the others will leave you alone, Chance never will. He hates you, Cullen."

"I'll not run . . . and this land is mine. I would put seed in the ground here, and grow crops, and build the place as Pa would have built it. If I leave all this behind his work was for nothing."

"His work was for you. It is you who are important, not the land."

"Are you so anxious to be rid of me?"

"No, but I want you alive."

Looking at her then I said something I had no right to say, no right even to think. "Where you are not—I would not feel alive."

Then I turned sharp around and walked into the sun-bright street, afraid of what I'd said, and not knowing why I'd said it, except that now it was said I knew it was the truest thing I had ever said.

Time was, any man who said such a thing and not one of her own kind would have been horsewhipped or called out. Yet I had said it who had no right of any kind to say that to such a girl, least of all to her.

There was no girl of her kind likely to have an interest in Cullen Baker. What was I but a big, loose-footed wandering man with no money and nothing to his name? And who was nobody, nor likely to be anybody.

Remembering the reflection I'd seen of myself in the window, I knew there was nothing in that big, shock-headed and raw-boned young man in a faded red wool shirt that would be likely to interest a Thorne of Blackthorne, or anybody who married with them. I was a man carried a pistol. Folks had no good to say of me, and mostly they were right. I was not as bad as they painted in most ways, but worse in some others. No hand to lie, I never drank either, although often they said I did, but I'd killed men in pistol fights and rode a hard trail over a lot of rough country.

How could a man driven to the swamps like a wounded wolf mean anything to such a girl? A man who had nothing to his name but three shirts and one pair of pants, a man who had drifted and rode and fought with the ragtag and bobtail of the West?

My mother had been quality and my father of good yeoman stock, but there'd been nothing else to the family. Pa had worked hard all his life, but he'd been unlucky. Fire had wiped out one home, and grasshoppers had taken the crop two years succeeding, and there were things happened no man can fight off, things that saddled us with debt.

Bob Lee was a knowing man, and Bob Lee looked me over and said, "I don't blame you, Cullen."

"What did he do?" Jack English wanted to know. "What aren't you blamin' him for? Because he whupped that Joel Reese? I'd have done it myself, if excuse had been offered. There never was a good thing about that man."

"You would have reason, Cullen," Bob Lee said. "I think she would go wherever you wanted to ride."

"Don't speak slighting of her, Bob."

"No such thing. I never spoke slighting of any woman, Cullen. Only she's in love with you, that one is."

"Of itself that's a slighting thing. What woman of sense could look at a man like me? How much time have I got, Bob? How much time have any of us? We've our enemies, you and me, and all of us, too. You have the Peacocks, and I have Chance Thorne, and then there's the Reconstruction people who've no use for any of us.

"I tell you, Bob, even if she'd have me, and there's no thinking of that, I'll have no woman crying over my blood-stained shirt, as I've often seen them cry."

We rode silent then, and after a bit Bob Lee said, "There's little sense in loving, Cullen. Love has a sense of its own and I expect often as not it's the best sense. Folks love with their blood and their flesh, Cullen, not with their brains. The sense of love is as deep as the water in Black Bayou, rich as the color of hyacinth. It makes no sense but to the people who love, and that's enough."

"Not for her and me, Bob Lee. And she has no such thought. It's only that we both liked her Uncle Will, I guess, and she may have sympathy for me."

"Have it your way," Bob Lee told me. "You've much to learn of women, Cullen."

Now no man likes to hear that. Each man believes he knows as much of women as the next, and in my time I'd known a few of them, and here and there women had been in love with me, or told it to me, but Katy Thorne was not likely to care for my kind of man, although she was a beautiful girl with a body that took a man's breath and embarrassed me to think on, not that I'm a man strange to women.

This day's work would bring trouble upon us all, but we had trouble already, and there was little they could do to us if we stayed to our swamps. Those carpetbagging soldiers weren't going to come into the swamp after us, not if they were in their right minds, but Colonel Amon Belser was a proud-walking man who would not like it said that he'd been made to look the fool, nor would he like to think that Bob Lee had been among the men, and Bob Lee with a price on his head.

What graveled us was the knowing that no Reconstruction was needed here. Texas had scarce been touched by the war, only men lost, and time taken from their work by it, but the carpetbaggers flocked to Texas because there was wealth to be had there and they wanted it.

As long as Throckmorton was governor he held them back, but when they'd thrown him out and put Davis in, we all knew we were in trouble. All state and local police had been disbanded and the Reconstruction were in power everywhere. Only we knew they wanted no newspaper talk, no publicity, just loot the state and get out, that was what they were thinking of.

Feeling had been intense up North when the war ended, but

right-thinking folks were already making themselves heard and the old abolitionist group of haters were losing out to the sober-minded who wished to preserve the Union and bring business back to where it had been. The Reconstruction people had been told to use discretion because, if they stirred up a fuss, feeling might turn fast against them.

"This Belser," Jack English said, "I've had an eye on him, and he sets store by Katy Thorne, and that Petraine woman, too. He'd like to go after the both of them, but there's men would kill him if he said a word to Katy Thorne, and as for Lacy Petraine, she needs no man to care for her."

It was the first talk I'd heard of Lacy Petraine, but right then the talk began, and I listened as I rode. She was new to the Five Counties, a New Orleans woman, but who'd lived else-where before that, and she had cash money, which was a rare thing.

She was a beauty, they said, and a dark, flashing kind of woman who carried herself as a lady and let no man think of her otherwise. She had bought local property from folks who wanted to go West, but what she had in mind or why she wanted to stay here, there was nobody could say.

On the island that night there was talk of Sam Barlow again. Matt Kirby had come to the island with the news of how Barlow had burned out a farm near San Augustine. He had killed a man there and run off his stock.

"If he comes up this away," Jack English suggested, "I say we run him off. I say we run him clean out of the country, or hang him."

If a man would just sit quiet and listen he could hear all the news right there on the island, for the men who sheltered there had friends everywhere, and word came to them by several means: a man riding by on the trails might leave a message in a hollow stump, or he might arrange the branches in a certain way, or the stones beside a trail. We had our ways of knowing things, even in the swamp, but Sam Barlow was a dangerous man to us, for if people began to believe we were doing the things he did we'd have no more friends among the folks out there. It was Reconstruction law wanted us, and none of us had done any harm to the folks who lived hereabouts.

Next day I saddled up that buckskin mule and rode down the island. There was only one place where a man might walk a horse or mule to the mainland and it took sharp attention and the right knowledge of just where to turn. There was an underwater ridge a man could ride, but well out from shore a man had to make a turn. It was a Caddo who showed me the way, and the first of the others had learned it from me . . . if a man made to ride on he'd be off in mighty deep water or in places, in mud that was like quicksand.

It was to Fairlea I rode. The distance was short, and I wanted to look about and see what my chances were to make something of the place. Actually, it was a better place than our home place, and one which Pa had picked up while land was cheap—for that matter it was still worth nothing. There were men with thousands of acres and no money at all, nor chance to get any. Crops brought nothing but a mere living, and cattle were killed for their hides and tallow.

The point of land I'd been considering was separated even from Fairlea except by a narrow lane along the bayou. There was some three hundred acres in the piece, but it lay in a half-dozen small fields, each walled by trees and bayous, the land lying like a letter S with an extra turn to it, and the bayous bordering it until it was all but an island. The lane along the trees ended in a gate on another lane, rarely used now, and by going through the gate and crossing the land one was on Fairlea proper.

There had once been a fine mansion house on the place, but it had burned to the ground one night before we ever came to the place, and the owner lost his family there, and after that sold to my father and went off to New Orleans. I believe part of the selling price was money owed to Pa for work done, and that during the spell when the owner had thoughts of rebuilding and going on, but the memories were too strong, and he finally would have none of it. So Fairlea fell to us for labor done and a little money.

The soil was good, and it would not be difficult to get in here, plow a field and seed it without anyone being the wiser.

The sound of the oncoming riders had been in my ears for a minute or more before I realized what it meant. Somebody was coming along the unused lane at the end of the property . . . now in the old days it had been a rare thing for anyone to ride that way, and by the looks of the lane, all grown to grass, it was a rarer thing even now.

If riders came this way it would be a good thing to know who they were and if they came often, but I'd more than an idea they were themselves not eager to be seen, choosing such a route as this, out of the way as it was.

It was a fine spring morning, and the sun was warm and lazy. Off in the bayous behind me somewhere a loon called, a mighty far and lonesome sound, at any time. Walking right up to the fence I lay that Spencer across the top rail with my hand over the action in such a way I could cock and fire almost in the same motion. And it was well I did just that because the man on the first horse was Sam Barlow.

He was a wide, thick-set man with a sight of hair on his chest, revealed by an open shirt. Barlow had the name of being a mighty dangerous man to come up against. He had fought as a guerrilla in the war, and had been a renegade since. Under the cover of fighting Reconstruction he was raiding, looting and murdering up and down the state, and into Louisiana and Arkansas. Folks had laid much of what he'd done on Bickerstaff, Bob Lee and some of the others, but Sam Barlow was a man known for cunning as well as being mighty mean, and he seemed always to know right where the Army was so he never did come up against them. Behind him right now there were about a dozen unkempt, dirty and mangy rascals who looked fit bait for the hangman.

About fifty feet from where I stood, Sam Barlow saw me and at first he stared like he couldn't believe what he was seeing. Then he lifted a hand to halt the little column, but by that time he was closer.

Taking a stub of cigar from his yellow teeth, he said, "Howdy! You live around here?"

Imperceptibly the muzzle of the carbine shifted until it covered Sam Barlow's chest. That carbine was down on the rail and partly hidden by brush . . . I don't figure he saw it.

"I live all around here."

"I'm Sam Barlow."

Now if he figured I was going to start shaking he was a mistaken man. Names never did scare me much, and I'd come up against some men who had bigger, tougher names than this here Barlow.

"I know who you are. Mighty far north, aren't you?"

Barlow returned that stub of cigar to his teeth. "I'm comin' further north. I like it here."

About that time he saw the carbine, and his lips tightened down and when his eyes lifted to mine they were wary, careful eyes. "Who are you?" he demanded.

"This is my country, Barlow. Stay the hell out of it."

Barlow was mad, I could see that. Moreover he wasn't so smart as I'd heard because he was going to buck that .56 caliber. He was going to bet me his life I'd miss. It was in his eyes, when a man behind him spoke. "Sam, this here is Cullen Baker."

That stopped him. Maybe they had heard about that killing a long time back at Fort Belknap, or maybe something else but, when he heard the name, Sam Barlow changed his mind and saved his life—because if that horse had moved a foot I was going to kill him.

He knew it, too. It is one thing to jump a horse at some

scared farmer. It is another thing to buck a man who can and will use a gun.

Same time, he'd no wish to lose face in front of his outfit, for the only way you lead a crowd like that was by being tougher, smarter, and maybe more brutal.

"I could use a man like you, Baker. I've heard tell of you."

"Stay out of this country, Barlow. You stay south or west of the Big Thicket. You come north of it and I'll take it unkind of you. Fact is, you come north of the Big Thicket and I'll kill you."

Well, sir, the planes in his face seemed to all flatten out and he made to spur his horse and when he did I cocked that .56 caliber. In that still air you could hear that carbine click as it cocked and Sam Barlow pulled his horse to a stand.

"Get out, Barlow, and take your outfit with you. There's country south of the Big Thicket for you, and if you open your mouth even once I'll spread you all over your saddle."

Sam Barlow was mad—he was mad clean through—and I didn't figure to even let him open his mouth because if he did he'd say something to try to make himself big with his crowd. It had probably been a long time since anybody told him to shut up and get out, but it had been done now, and no mistake.

They would be back, I could bet on that. Sam Barlow could not afford to take water from any man, but he would think awhile before he came back, and he would do some planning, but if he stayed south of Lake Caddo then Katy Thorne would be safe.

"And that was what you were thinking about," I told myself. "You've heard of Barlow's ways with women."

Turning around then I saw four riders coming up the field toward me, and they were well spread out, but they were Matt Kirby, Bickerstaff and Bill Longley. On the far wing of the four was Bob Lee.

"Sam Barlow backed down," Kirby was saying. "He backed down cold."

"Means nothing," I said, "I had him dead to rights. And that .56 makes quite a hole."

"They'll come back." Bob Lee was a serious thinking man. He was looking past the moment, and he could see what it was we'd have to expect.

"Why, then," Bill Longley was grinning, "we shouldn't keep them waiting. We should go after them, Bob. We should go right down into the Thicket after them."

They were waiting for me, but when I reached a hand for the pommel of the mule's saddle I was thinking, "You've got to find a way to get a gun into action faster, Cullen Baker. Else they'll come up on you some time. You've got to learn how to get a Colt into action faster than any man would ever believe possible. You've got to think out how they might approach you and what you'll do in case.

"Otherwise they'll surely kill you."

THREE

A pistol was carried in a holster or thrust into the waistband.
The habit of carrying pistols on the hip had not developed
to any extent, and hand guns were only becoming common
now. The Dragoon and Walker Colts were too heavy for comfort. Usually, until now a pistol had been carried on the saddle,
yet for a man who needed a weapon that could be brought
swiftly into action, the pistol was the best.

Long ago at Fort Belknap I'd traded several surplus rifles for
a pistol. The rifles were of the muzzle-loading variety then
being sold to Indians, and which I'd won gambling.

That was the time a soldier taught me the Army method of
loading the Dragoon Colt, when afoot or riding horseback, and
he had drilled me until I'd become far more proficient than the
average cavalryman ever became. Doing things with my hands
had always been easy for me—I had the knack. Maybe that was
because I'd worked with my hands since a boy, braiding raw-
hide ropes, splicing ropes we used on the farm, doing what
needs to be done. So more than most, I was handy with a
pistol, and felt right at home with it.

No pistol would be any use to a man in trouble unless it was out and shooting, so the problem was getting the pistol into action, then firing accurately and with speed.

That last wasn't going to figure as troublesome. At Fort Belknap when I hung around there I'd done a sight of shooting with soldiers and proved then that what they could do I could do better. My shooting was better than any of them, and for some time I'd kept myself in money winning bets on shooting with both rifle and pistols.

Back on the island that night after the meeting with Sam Barlow I stretched out on a grassy bank just at the edge of the firelight and did some serious thinking. It was a problem I had to solve, and I'd never figured myself for too much of a thinker, but I do say I was persistent. I mean I could hold to an idea and plug away at it and size it up from all angles until it began to make sense.

After all, what's there to thinking? The way I figure it there was so much a body could do with a mind. You could take the various possibilities and line them all up, and then eliminate the ones that weren't practical. The main idea was to stay with an idea until all the possibilities were worked out.

Thinking was something I worked at like a prospector washing out gold. I'd take me a brain full of the coarse gravel of ideas and sift it down until the gold remained. Only sometimes I worked a long time and came up with no color showing at all.

That pistol would be in my waistband. That way I could lay a quick hand on it. What I needed was to get that pistol out and shooting, and I'd have to be prepared for a target from any direction. I wasn't to be able to shoot just where I wanted to.

This was easier said than done. Getting up I walked off down a path where I could be alone and unobserved. Standing in a little clearing I drew the gun and aimed at a mark—too slow.

Yet why should a man aim? When I point my finger at something I just point directly at the object, so why not the same thing with a pistol? And if a man could fire from wherever he had his gun, so much the better. It would have the advantage of the unexpected, and that was a primary concern. Of course, I'd have to be careful of that trigger squeeze. A man could pull his gun barrel out of line with the target if he gave it just a might too much. Still, I'd mostly be shooting from close up, and the target would be a man's body. I'd waste no time on head shots.

Whoever came against me would surely have help, and it was almost as sure that I'd be alone. Therefore if my gun was in action quicker then I might win with the first shot.

Nine out of ten fist fights are won with the first blow, so why not a gun battle with the first shot?

The problem was to get that gun out fast. . . .

Right then I started to practice, drawing that pistol again and again, and sighting at whatever mark showed. The front sight had a way of snagging on my shirttail or beltband, so I would file that off. A thin white line on the muzzle would do most as good for close work, anyway.

The problem then was to draw swiftly, to fire at once, and above all to make the first shot count.

There was no use to waste ammunition firing until I'd developed some skill, and until I'd practiced turning and aiming at targets to the side or behind me. The problem here was to focus on the target at once and let the gun muzzle go where the eyes went.

Right then I started, drawing fifty times by actual count, trying to break the draw down to its actual fundamentals. So I started trying to find the quickest and smoothest ways of grasping the gun—grasp counted for very much, and that first grip must be sure, clean and positive. If that was done half the problem was solved, for then the gun came up in line and didn't jump when the trigger was squeezed.

At daybreak the next morning I walked down to the far end of the island where nobody could see what I was doing and I practiced for three hours. After three hours I rested and thought about it for thirty minutes and then returned to work. My life depended on my success so I wasn't about to waste time. So I worked on steadily through the afternoon.

If the elbow was held loosely against the hip or the body above the hip my position seemed a little better, and the pistol could be pointed by the whole body.

The art of drawing a gun fast had never been developed by anyone. Until now there had been no particular reason for developing any such skill, for men fought duels on carefully paced-off ground, or they went looking for one another, gun in hand. Usually, disputes were settled by carefully arranged duels with gun, knife or sword. Moreover, the first successful repeating pistol made in any quantity was the Walker Colt, invented by Samuel Colt and designed for the Texas Rangers by order of Walker. But like the Dragoon Colt, it was heavy.

And the fast draw was of advantage only to a man who might expect attack at any time, from any direction.

That first day I worked seven hours, until my hand was sore and I was some tired out. But I had a feeling that I'd hit on something new, and that what I was doing would work in practice, and that's the test of any idea.

Next day I rode to Fairlea and, with a team borrowed from a farmer who'd known Pa, I started breaking ground. After staying away for a few days so as to give nobody a chance for an ambush, I returned again. Each time that I came back to Fairlea I scouted all around before showing myself in the open. The chances were that Sam Barlow had no idea the field belonged to me, and most likely assumed I was merely passing through.

On the fourth day I finished my plowing, and later I dragged the field and planted my corn.

When I'd come back to Texas I'd had a little money, but most of it went to pay for the seed corn.

Time to time I'd find myself thinking of Katy Thorne, although I knew I'd no business thinking of her. But I'd keep bringing to mind the way her face looked in the candlelight, and how good it felt to be sitting in a home, with comfort around me and the sound of a woman moving about the house. But much as I wanted to, I stayed away from Blackthorne. I'd no desire to go to stirring up a lot of wishing that I'd no business with. I was a man with nothing, and with small prospects of living out the summer. Only I figured to have my say on that last point. I had most unfriendly ideas about dying, particularly from a gunshot by that riffraff that followed Reconstruction.

There had been no further forays by Sam Barlow into our neck of the woods. That country from Lake Caddo to the Oklahoma-Arkansas line he'd avoided. Bob Lee, however, and some of the other had ridden out and had themselves some gun talk with Reconstruction soldiers, in which they came off very well and the soldiers not so good.

The Reconstruction Act of 1867, followed by the removal of Governor Throckmorton from office, had been accepted by most Texans as another declaration of war. The carpetbaggers and Union Leaguers had come to Texas to get rich quick, and most of them were folks of low integrity and no morals to speak of. Here and there, however, to give them their just due, there would be one who amounted to something, and a few of these stayed on in Texas to become valued citizens. But they were mighty scarce.

Mostly those who came south were the wrong ones. They allied themselves with folks of the same kind in Texas, and they figured to force their will on us by shooting and burning which only stiffened resistance and drove many a good man into the swamps or the thickets, and most of us who took to the thickets had to learn to use our guns to live.

That section of East Texas was thickly forested with piney woods where even then folks had started a few small lumber operations, and here and there where the woods had been cleared out folks had started farming or grazing a few cows.

Unless you've seen an East Texas thicket you surely can't imagine what they're like—millions of acres covered by a dense, junglelike growth of pine, dogwood, chinquapin, elderberry, myrtle, blackjack and prickly pear. Above all, prickly pear. There was cat's-claw, of course, and even ferns as tall as trees and wild orchids, but all through it was a growth of tall, old prickly pear with spines that would rip a man's eyes out, and in places made a wall nothing could get through.

The Big Thicket to the south was over a hundred miles long and about fifty wide, but there were other thickets such as Mustang, Jernigan, and Blackjack Thicket, just to name a few. Here and there among the thickets there were streams of waterholes, sometimes even good-sized ponds or small lakes, teeming with fish. There was a lot of wild game, and some of the most vicious wild cattle a man ever came across. There were wild cattle in there that would stalk a man like a cougar stalks a heifer, mean as all get out.

During the Shelbyville war between the Regulators and the Moderators these thickets and the swamps along the Sulphur had offered shelter for the fighting men and refugees as well as for outlaws from the Natchez or Trammel Traces. Growing up in those swamps and thickets, I probably knew as much about them as any one man . . . it would take a lifetime to know it all, believe me.

Few rivers on earth could twist and turn more than the Sulphur Fork of the Red. And few offered so great a variety of hiding places as did the curves, bends, islands and swamps of the Sulphur. When in the southern part of the area the boys hid out on the island in the Lake Caddo swamps, but farther north, not too far from Boston or the Arkansas line, there were hide-outs at McFarland Island between the circle of Piney Lake, Spring Lake and the Sulphur itself. And there were two hide-outs in the Devil's Den region between the Sulphur River and Bell's Slough. Of course, there were others, some known to one group, some to another, but maybe I was the only one

who knew them all, or so I figured. And most of them I'd
learned from my friends, the Caddoes.

Bob Lee and the others left me alone. This was a time when
nobody catered much to folks asking questions and a man's
business was figured to be his own. Only sometimes the boys
would get to riding me.

"Got himself a girl," Matt Kirby suggested.

"He's sparkin' that widow," Jack English said. "Most ever'body
else is tryin'."

"Makes a man right uncomfortable, the way she looks at him
sometimes," Bickerstaff told them. "She's all woman that one.
Take a sight of man to keep her inside the fence."

It was Lacy Petraine of whom they talked. She was the
subject of more talk than any woman I ever did see. Mostly
they called her "that New Orleans woman," or "the widow"
like that country wasn't full of widows, those times. But when a
woman who looks like she does comes into a broke country
carrying a sack full of hard cash, there's sure to be talk.

Chance Thorne was taking some rides, too. From time to
time I heard talk of his being seen around the country, yet he
rode quite a ways south, and what down there could be important to him? Could be he was sparking some woman himself,
yet Chance was a man not likely to ride far out of his way for
any woman, and who did few things without a mighty big
reason. Who was south that was so important to him?

When the idea came it sort of shocked me into sitting straight
up. Bob Lee turned sharp around, afraid I'd heard something
that spelled trouble. "What is it, Cull?"

"Had a mite of an idea." I wrapped my arms around my
knees. "Bill," I asked Longley, "would you do something for
me?"

"You just give it a name."

"Try to find out where Chance goes on those rides."

Longley considered it. "You've got an idea where he goes?"

"I'm guessing, but I'd say the Big Thicket."

"Sam Barlow's country," Bickerstaff objected. "He wouldn't go there."

"Maybe."

Bob Lee took a stick from the fire to light his cigar. "You think he's the one who's been tipping off Sam Barlow about the Army?" He looked at me with one of those quick, sharp glances of his. "You don't like the man. You could be prejudiced."

"Might be," I admitted slowly. "It could be, of course, but I just don't believe I am, not to interfere with my judgment. Chance is a thinking man, a mighty thinking man when it comes to what is best for Chance. His side of the family were well-off, but never so much as the rest of the Thornes, and that never did set well with him. I believe he's out to make himself some money and I think he'd play all sides to do it."

Two days later when I was chopping weeds out of my cornfield there was a rider in the lane. The Spencer was leaning against a tree not too far off and I walked over to it, but when the rider showed up it was the horse that got me, not the rider.

"I am not flattered, Mr. Baker," she said.

When she spoke it was in a low, confidential voice, and I looked up into the eyes of the most beautiful woman I'd ever seen. I knew right off it was that New Orleans woman, Lacy Petraine.

"Beautiful horse," I told her.

Her expression did not change. "Yes, he is a fine animal. So are you, Mr. Baker."

That was direct talk and I looked at her, measuring what I saw, and what this woman had she wasn't pretending she didn't have. It was there, all right. Whatever else she was she was like they said, she was all woman.

"This was the sort of horse I was thinking about," I said thoughtfully.

"I came here to talk to you about a job, Mr. Baker."

"I'm not hiring anybody," I said. "I can't afford it."

She ignored it. "I need a man—"

"Most women do," I told her innocently.

Her lips tightened. "Mr. Baker, apparently I am wasting my time. I heard of your trouble with the Reconstruction people and they are a group with whom I have some influence. If you accept the job I have for you, I can promise you that you will no longer be annoyed."

She was mad, but she wasn't backing off. Maybe I don't have any clothes to speak of, and I'm not much at dancing, but when I see that look in a woman's eyes I take it she's not thinking of playing whist.

"Mr. Baker, I am buying property. I sometimes carry a little money, and I need a man who can ride with me whom people respect and who can use a gun. With Sam Barlow and his kind I no longer feel safe."

"You'd be better off to talk to Colonel Belser. He would be glad to provide an escort, or do it himself."

"He offered, but I want no connection with him or what he represents. You see, Mr. Baker, I intend to make my home here, and I can imagine it will be difficult for those who were too friendly with the carpetbaggers when the carpetbaggers are gone."

"Somebody should tell that to Chance Thorne."

Putting a hand on the fence at a place where there was no brush, I vaulted it and walked over to her. She sat her horse watching me with a quirt in her hand and a pistol in a saddle scabbard, but I walked around the horse, sizing it up. I always had a good eye for horse flesh—but I was not missing the woman either.

When I was around on the other side I put my hand up as if to reach for her but just caressed the horse. She was looking at me, and I'll give her this, she wasn't scary. In such a position, lonely like it was, most women would have been. I figure she had an idea she could handle whatever showed up, any way she chose to handle it.

"If you are interested in fine horse," she said, "you should work for me. I have several of the very best."

"How'd you know to find me here?"

"You had been described to me, and I was riding by. I am interested in property, Mr. Baker, and have been looking for something I can buy."

"I am not for sale."

She got mad then, really mad. "You flatter yourself, Mr. Baker. I assure you, any interest I had in your working for me is ended."

She rode away, her back rigid with anger, but when I walked back to my hoe the zest for work was gone. No question about it, I'd acted like a country bumpkin, which was what I was, only I needn't have acted it. And she was a sight of woman— most woman I'd seen in one package for a long time. The sort of woman who'd give a man all he'd ask for, and then some.

Hiding the hoe I mounted my mule and rode back into the swamp and dismounting in a quiet place I started working with the pistol. When the sweat was streaming from me and my hand was getting sore again, I let up. But it had seemed to be coming faster, with less lost motion and a surer grasp of the gun on that first grab. It had to be like that, for if danger came there would be no room for failure.

Seeing Lacy Petraine brought Katy Thorne to mind. Katy didn't have the flesh of that New Orleans woman, but her beauty was just as great. She had a way of carrying herself, cool, poised, and graceful . . . I must find some excuse for seeing Katy.

It was Matt Kirby who knew about Lacy Petraine. Or as much as anybody knew about her. She looked twenty-three or -four, but the way Matt figured it she just had to be at least six years older. Her Pa had owned a plantation near New Orleans, the way Matt had it, and Lacy was of French-Spanish-Irish ancestry, but by the time she was a girl her father had gambled away most of what they had, and she had moved into New

Orleans with her father. The year she was sixteen he had died of yellow fever, and she married an Irish gambler named Terence O'Donnell.

He was, according to Matt, a gentleman. He was thirty-two when she married him, handsome, shrewd, and as skillful and successful at gambling as her Pa had been otherwise.

They left New Orleans for Atlanta, and later Matt heard tell of her in Charleston, Richmond and New York. Some said she had been in Havana, too. Then one night on a riverboat Terence dealt the wrong card to the wrong man, was challenged and killed. He left his young wife with a knowledge of cards and fourteen thousand dollars in money.

At eighteen she took off for Europe with two Negro girls for slaves and a big Negro man who was nearly sixty but mule-strong. Next two years she lived in Paris, London, Vienna, Rome, Venice and Madrid, and then she'd been in some sort of a mixup with a man, or so Matt had it from her maid. A love affair that turned out wrong, from what he said. She married André Petraine who was the bastard son of a prominent Frenchman. André tried to blackmail his father and was murdered, quick and simple. Same night they gave Lacy passage to New York and the suggestion she go there and stay.

On the way back some men taught her to play poker, and lost three thousand dollars doing it. Supplying money to an old friend of O'Donnell's, she opened a gambling house in Charleston. Before the war began she sold the gambling house and invested in cotton, sold it well in London and remained there during most of the war.

Matt Kirby had served during part of the war with the friend who had operated her Charleston place, and it was from him that he had pieced together much of the story. Without allegiance to anyone she had returned with sufficient cash to buy land, and it was East Texas she chose, feeling that with Reconstruction sure to go out in a few years she could be one of the wealthiest women in that area.

69

It was a good scheme, the way Kirby had it, and the way it seemed to figure out. We'd heard around that she was buying land, and that she wasn't a bit upset by the Barlow raids, or any other for that matter. The more folks were frightened the more apt they would be to sell out for a cheap price. According to all accounts she was a woman who knew what she wanted and how to get it.

One thing started me to wondering about how much she wanted me to work for her and how much she might have other ideas in mind. She owned the old Drummond place which adjoined Fairlea on the north, and she owned another farm south of my place.

No matter. I'd my own plans to think of, and with a crop in the ground I could start looking farther ahead. There were occasional drives of cattle to Shreveport or Sedalia, and in the Thickets there were thousands of head, unbranded, and whose ownership would be impossible to trace. Deep in the swamp, under the dark-leaved cypress and the hanging moss, I thought it out, figured just how it could be done, and how it had to be done. And no day went by when I did not practice with a gun.

One night, we were sitting around the fire when suddenly out in the swamp, a fish jumped. We all knew the sound yet the suddenness of it caught us by surprise and in an instant there was nobody about the fire, nothing but the fire burning alone, the empty beds and saddles. In the thick shade of a cypress I looked down at the pistol in my hand and could not remember drawing it.

So that was the way it was then. I was learning, all right, I was faster, much faster.

Nobody moved. Here and there a rifle barrel gleamed in the brush around the clearing while we listened, and then we heard another noise, not of the swamp. A rider was coming who knew the way to come. We waited in the shadows, almost counting the steps. When the rider came into the circle of light it was Matt Kirby.

He was a broad, solid man with a wide face and jaw, a quiet man who drank too much, yet always managed to be where the soldiers were not. He dismounted and went to the fire, pouring black coffee into a smoke-blackened tin cup.

"Raid south of here," he said as we started to come in, "and a woman killed. They say Cullen done it."

"There it is, Cull," Longley said. "They'll mean it now."

"Three posses out," Kirby said. "That's why I hightailed it back here. The orders are to shoot to kill, and if you're taken alive, to hang you."

"That would be Barlow," I said. "I told him to stay away from here."

Bickerstaff got up. "Cullen, you've got to run. Even this place isn't safe."

"I'll stay."

"We can go to Devil's Den," Lee suggested. "It's farther north and no way they could find us there."

Devil's Den was one of the best places, difficult to get at, and easy to defend. No posse in their right minds would attempt to even come near the place.

"You go ahead," I told them. "I'm going into the Big Thicket."

They all sat around looking at me, trying to see what it was in my mind. All I knew was Sam Barlow was there and the time had come for a killing, for an old-fashioned gut-shooting. I was going to see Sam Barlow. I was going to read him from the Scriptures.

"Heard something else," Kirby said. "There's a dozen riders camped on Blackthorne. They pulled in there while I was coming across country."

If these were Barlow's men on Blackthorne, and I had no idea who else they might be, Katy was in trouble. Getting up I walked to my mule and began to saddle up. It might be too late, even now.

71

Longley came over to me where I was cinching up. "What's bitin' you, Cull? You takin' off like a sca'ed pa'tridge?"

"Katy Thorne and her aunt live alone on Blackthorne."

"You set store by that gal?"

"I do."

"Then you just hold up while I get my saddle."

Bob Lee came up to his horse packing his saddle under his arm. "I take it mighty hard, you fixing to ride off into trouble alone, Cull. A man would think you had no friends."

"I'm obliged."

Watching them saddle up gave me a strange, warm, odd sort of feeling. There had not been many friends for me during the years I'd ridden the country, or wherever I lived, and there are fewer friends when trouble raises its hand.

Not that I deserved friends. I'd lived too much alone and with a chip on my shoulder, always wanting friendship but wary of folks, fearful of what might come of trying friendship. Thing is, if a man wants friends he's got to be friendly. Takes a man a sight of time to learn the simplest things, it seems.

Matt Kirby switched his saddle to Bickerstaff's spare horse, and when we rode out of there I felt better than any king with an army at his back, for these were good men who rode beside me, and like myself they were men driven to the wall with only ourselves to fight for, and the things in which we believed. If it was Sam Barlow on Blackthorne he'd better make himself scarce before we got there or he'd be planted in that swampy ground.

No moon lit the sky when we rode down the dark lanes, the sound of our horses' hoofs hard upon the roads, or whispering through the grassy fields, but we needed no moon for we were men to whom darkness was a friend. We rode dark horses and our clothes were dark, with no white shirts and no ornaments on our saddles or anything to make a target for a seeing man.

"They'll take time to settle in camp," Kirby said, reassuring me. "They'll be under the big trees between the house and the river."

The house they spoke of was the big house, Blackthorne itself, and some three hundred yards from Will's old place where Katy was . . . and Blackthorne closed these many months now, closed and still. No doubt they figured to loot the big house, and it would be a rich place to take, bank on that.

I cared just nothing for what they took from Blackthorne, but if Katy was touched, or even if they talked rough to her or threatened her, I'd bury Sam Barlow deep. For I was a man with one thought nor anything to lose but my life, which might be called a wasted thing, even now.

There was no moon when we started, but by the time we turned into the grass lane that led to a broken-down fence the moon was chinning itself on the horizon trees, and the vague light in the sky was lowering itself through the trees but little enough of it was showing when we rode into the orchard and up through the aisle between the trees. With luck we would arrive unseen and unheard.

It was very still, with only the frogs croaking, but when we were but halfway through the big orchard we heard drunken voices near Will's house and then a pounding on the door. Looked like we'd arrived right on time.

"Open up! Open up in there or we'll bust the door!"

Inside me something started to swell and grow, and I knew what it was because I'd felt it before, the black angry rage, the choking fury that rose inside me until it filled me with a roaring anger, and then a strange and frightening coldness. I knew myself, and was frightened at these rages of mine, and fought them down, but not now.

From inside the house we heard Katy speak, heard faintly as we walked our horses on the grass of the long untouched orchard. "Go away! Go, or I'll shoot!"

"Now you see here," one of the men called persuasively, "you can't shoot us all and we sure enough aim to come in.

73

Now you be a good girl and open that door. You can't shoot us all."

Now the night was still, like I said, and by that time we were right up to the house, and so when the sound of his voice died I spoke quiet but clear enough. "She can't shoot you all," I said. "But *we* can."

You might say there was a change you could feel. You might say these were startled men, and if you said it, you'd be right. Nobody much bothered Barlow men, they'd had their own way about things, but now they were called upon by a voice from the night.

These men standing there before that house where I'd been received in friendship were killers and rapers of women, they were horse thieves, deserters and rascals, and bad as I might be, I'd never touched the level of such scum as these.

"Stay out of this, whoever you are, and you won't get hurt."

Why, I was mad. I was mad and ugly and I laughed, and I am afraid it was not a good laugh. "Are you Barlow men?" I asked.

"We are, and what of it?"

"I told Barlow to stay the hell out of this country. You want to leave now or be buried here?"

The moon was behind the trees, but the light filtered through the cypresses and fell across the door of the house where Katy lived, and the Barlow men stood in the vague light of the coming moon, but we were scattered out on the edge of the orchard, its blackness behind us, and they could see nothing, but could hear a voice only.

There was muttering among them, uneasiness, too. They did not like it, but there might be only one man, and I saw a rifle move.

My Spencer was low across the saddle and on the body of a man standing nearest the door, with a streak of light from a shutter falling across him. I could see a vest pocket and the gray of a lighter shirt, and when that rifle moved I shot him in the stomach.

Along the front of the orchard to the right of me there was a rippling spatter of sound, of hard sound, and I saw men falling and then I was riding in. Going in I held on a man's skull knowing it was a chancy shot, but liking the target, and saw the man go down as the Spencer fired not three feet from his skull as I rode up to him.

The night was roaring with gunfire, and the Barlow men scattered and fell, and rose to rush on and staggered, then fell again. It was sudden, and it was complete and we saw one wounded man rolling on the ground trying to put out the fire the bullet had started on his shirt front. That black powder had a way of throwing grains—I'd seen men tattooed with it.

Their camp was beyond the big house and we rode through the trees on a dead run, weaving among them, shouting rebel yells and shooting at everything that moved in the flickering light among the tree trunks and the shrubs and the moonlight.

Then we saw their fire and a man running from it, and Bill Longley fired and the man stumbled and sprawled forward, falling in flight like a partridge landing, and then he started to get up and three bullets nailed him to the dark earth where he dug in his fingers and died, red blood joining the black earth beneath him.

"Good shot," I said, "we'll go goose-hunting this fall."

We swung down and Bickerstaff turned Bill's dead man over and there were finger-nail scratches on his face. This could be the man who had raped and killed the woman of whom we'd heard, or some other woman.

There were two Dragoon Colts in the camp and a Henry rifle which was brand- spanking-new, two old muskets and a Ballard rifle. There was also coffee, sugar, rice and some baked bread. We took it all, being hunted men who found it hard to get food. One of the Colts I took myself and tossed the other to Longley. Lee took the Ballard rifle.

When we walked our horses back across the lawn there was a moment when I drew in my mule to look up at the big house. "A long time ago," I told Lee, "they used to dance here. On the nights when they'd have a ball sometimes I'd watch from out in the trees. Folks would come up in their fine carriages, and they'd get out and go up the steps, and there'd be music from inside the house."

"Never see the like again," Bob Lee said soberly. "It was another world."

It was true enough, but I who had been no part of it regretted it.

The door was open when we pulled up and Katy was kneeling beside the body of a man who was badly hurt. She stood up as we drew near. "Will you help me get this man into a bed?"

"He was goin' to bust in on you, ma'am," Bickerstaff said. "He's better off dead. That's a mean man you've got there."

"You should have killed him then. I'll let no man die at my door, not even a wolf."

We carried him in and bedded him down, and Katy put water on the fire. We'd come off well, not a scratch among us, for our attack had been too sudden and they'd had no time to do anything but get off quick, unaimed shots in hopes they'd land.

Under the trees we found three dead men to add to the one killed by the door, and another badly wounded. At least two more men were wounded and out in the grass, and the way I figured it there was another dead man out there, and we'd best go hunting him.

"Sam Barlow won't like it," Matt Kirby was lighting his pipe. "I tell you he won't."

"He'll come," Bickerstaff said. "He'll come soon, I'm thinking."

"Then he'd better make it soon," I told them, "because if he doesn't I'll go hunting him."

"Keep the shovel after we've buried these others," I said,

"because I'm going to dig Barlow a grave at the Corners. I'll dig the grave and put up a marker and leave it open for him."

Longley chuckled. "Now there's a thought, and I'd give a year of my life to see his face when he heard of it. I'll throw dirt from that grave myself, Cullen, and be proud to hold the shovel."

The wounded man looked at Cullen Baker. "You'll dig the grave for your own body, whoever you are. Barlow will kill you for this."

"Whoever I am? The name is Cullen Baker, and I'll have the hide of any man who raises a hand against Katy Thorne."

Startled, the wounded man turned his head sharply toward Katy. "You're a *Thorne?*" He was shocked. "Relative to Chance?"

"His sister-in-law."

"Good God!" The wounded man's fear was a frightening thing. "Barlow will have my hide for this!"

"Barlow is a friend of Chance, is that it?" I asked.

Katy glanced at me sharply, but the wounded man merely stared at the ceiling and would say nothing more.

We dug the grave by moonlight as one should dig the grave of such a man, and we finished as the moon was setting behind the trees, and over the open grave we posted a marker with the words burned deep with a branding iron.

HERE LIES SAM BARLOW
COWARD
THIEF
MURDERER
KILLED BY CULLEN BAKER

Before the sun was three hours old the marker at the Corners had been seen by a dozen men and, the love of a good story being what it is, before sundown they were telling it in Lufkin to the south and Boston to the north.

And in the swamps along the Sulphur where hard men

relished a hard joke, the men in the hide-outs were chuckling and awaiting the fireworks.

And in the Big Thicket the story came to Sam Barlow, and they tell me his fury was a thing to see. They tell me that he raged and ranted and swore, but in the end he settled down into something cold and dangerous, and the men who heard such things and carried the news warned me: "Be careful man, he must kill you now or leave the country. He'll be coming north when you least expect."

And in the clearing back of my cornfield at Fairlea I practiced with the Colt, and it came to my hand with smoothness now, and it came with ease, and the muzzle found the target like a living thing. They could come when they wished, for I was ready now.

FOUR

My corn was growing tall when I rode again to the house of Katy Thorne. It had become a place I could not leave alone, nor my quiet talks with her, nor the good coffee in the candlelight. There was a softness in me that I'd nigh forgotten, and I'd sit tipped back in my chair watching her move about the room, listening to the rustle of her skirts, and at times talking to Aunt Flo.

It was a strange thing for me, a hard man grown accustomed to hard ways, to talk with this maiden lady and to Katy, but the house had a warmth for me that I liked. I knew I was not the only visitor, for Katy Thorne had a way with people, and even Chance came at times, although unwelcome I knew. And there was another, a man I'd not met, named Thomas Warren, and a teacher in a school not far away.

He was a stiff young man who rode uncomfortably in the saddle and who had a high-nosed way about him that drew some joking from the boys in the swamps who had seen him about. Yet he had much talk of books that Katy hungered for, and it was something I could not give her. I read whatever came to hand, but it was little enough, and mainly old newspapers and sometimes a magazine.

It was growing faintly yellow around the trees when I came again to the house of Katy Thorne. It was early, but there was smoke from the chimney, and knowing Aunt Flo was a late riser I surmised it must be Katy herself who was up and about.

She saw me coming and opened the door. "Put your horse away. I have breakfast ready."

It was a welcome thing, for I had worked until after dark the night before, and was too tired to prepare food for myself, so I'd dumped water over me from the well and sponged off and gone at once to bed.

These days I was staying at times in the old family house, but not often, and usually in the swamps, but I was a man wary of surprise, and not wanting to travel the same trail too often, so I shifted about and kept myself out of the way and out of sight.

There had been no trouble yet with the Reconstruction people, although there was talk of my arrest for taking the guns from Colonel Belser, in Jefferson. There'd been a note I sent him in which I protested any claim he had to the weapons, for his men taking mine from me.

There was a small shed in the orchard where I stabled my horse these days, and kept oats or corn for it, and some hay. There were two doors at opposite ends and the place was hidden in vines and behind a row of trees, and not many knew it was there. A great wisteria vine had grown over it, and the place had not been used in so many years that even those who knew the place had almost forgotten it.

Katy was at the door when I came, and there was worry in her eyes. "They may come for you, Cullen. It is a worrisome thing. Thomas was saying the other night that people want you arrested."

"People?"

80

"Some of those he speaks to, the farmers north of here, and the Reconstruction people."

"I've no doubt of it. There will always be some who will not like me. It is the old story of the dog with the bad name. There are some who blame me for anything Barlow does, or anything done by drifting renegades. I am sorry, Katy, but I warned you of what people would say."

She smiled at me. "Since when has the countryside told a Thorne who is acceptable and who is not? You will come when you like, Cullen, and stay as long as you like."

"Well, then. You've no worry right now about them coming upon me. There's a man on the highroad and another in the lane. We'll have warning enough."

Aunt Flo was in the bedroom with the wounded man. His recovery had been slow, and for a time it was doubtful that he would recover at all. Now, slowly, he was coming around.

Katy noticed the guns at my belt. "Must you always wear those?"

"Would you have me ride without them, Katy? They're as necessary to me as hairpins to you, or the ring on your finger, more so, because they are my life itself. I live by them, and perhaps shall die by them, but while I live they must never be far from my hand.

"There's a fine, strong feeling in the butt of a gun, Katy, for it's a man's weapon, but a gun is meant for death, and is not to be treated lightly or as a toy. A gun is like a woman or a horse, and not to be handled by a man who doesn't understand it."

"You understand women, then?"

"Only that like a fine pistol they must be handled gently or they're apt to explode." I grinned at her. "You know the swamps are no place to learn of women."

"How about those Western lands? I've heard stories of you out there, and in the Mormon country. Did you have three wives out there?"

81

"Not one, Katy. Not even a small, quiet one. I'd a horse and a gun and little else."

She was pouring coffee then and she put down the pot and said, "Cullen, why don't you leave here? Why don't you go some place you won't be needing a gun? Are you always to live like this?"

"Can I give up all this, Katy, and make Pa's life a useless thing? And if I run this time, who is to say when I shall have to run again? And when shall I stop running? My father played to ill luck all his life, yet at the end he had this land, and little as land in Texas is worth, it was all he had, and it was left to me. And here I shall stay."

"There is hatred for you here, Cullen. Even the good people fear you. No matter what is to come, I am afraid they would never trust you or want you here."

The gloom was on me then for I knew the truth of what she said, and felt deep within me a sense of being fated for ill things.

"They are right to want to kill me," I said at last, "for there is a difference in me, and deep within every animal there is a need to kill what is different. There is always the feeling that what is different may expose them all to danger.

"When I came here as a stranger they attacked me because I was a stranger and seemed vulnerable. They believed me weak because I was alone, and I was not weak for the very reason that I was alone."

"You must leave. It is the only way."

"Maybe they are right to kill me," I repeated, captured by the trend of my thinking. "Wild animals often kill animals that are different, a white wolf among gray wolves must be a terrible fighter to survive, for their instinct is to kill, perhaps because a white wolf can be seen farther and may bring danger to the pack."

"Will Sam Barlow come looking for you?"

"He will. He must come. Stay clear of me, Katy. I'm a man

who attracts trouble. And I must stay away from you, for I'll surely bring grief to you, and danger."

"You have saved me from danger."

"Yes . . . and if I am killed I want you to have Fairlea, and the crop I planted there."

She looked at me in sudden surprise. "You've planted a crop? How could you?"

"It was the first thing I did. When I came back here it was to make a new life, and I have not wished for trouble. They brought it to me, Chance first, and then Barlow, and those others with the loose tongues who talk of me as an outlaw and a bad one.

"The love of the land is in me, Katy, and it is all I have. Without it all I have is a horse and a gun and a will to fight. I'm as free as one of those soldiers of fortune of the free companies who sold their services to kings in the old days. Yet if there is anything will save me from what I am, it is the land. I am a man of blood and fury, Katy, perhaps it's the Black Irish in me, and if there is peace for me it will be on the land."

"If you harvest your crop, what then?"

"I'll store it for feed, and then with some of the others we'll round up wild cattle from the thickets and drive them off for sale in the north. With what cash I get I shall buy a stallion and a couple of good mares and start breeding horses. It is a thing I have been wanting to do." Pausing, I stared at the candle flame. "And I'll do it, too, if I am not killed."

"That isn't like you, Cullen, to speak of dying."

"It is though. I live with it. I am not one of those fools who believe it is always the other man who is killed by accident or a gun. I know it can happen to me, it can happen to anyone, at any time. Anyone who takes an unnecessary risk is a fool, and I don't want to die when I haven't lived."

"Go away, Cullen," she pleaded, "go West, or anywhere. You would not be running away, and if you live you will have

83

defeated them. And what does it matter what they believe, anyway?"

At the door, when it was almost noon, I told her, "You shouldn't waste time on me. I'm no good."

"If you think that," she replied sharply, "others will think it. Respect begins with self-respect."

"You know you're right?" I told her. "You're damned right."

At the shed I led out the horse I was riding today, giving my mule a chance to rest. The mule was tough and seemed willing to go for hours on little food and less sleep, but nothing can stand up to that, and I must be in shape for a fast and long run, so the mule took turns now with a spare horse of Bickerstaff's.

When I reached Jack English who waited in the lane, we rode to the highway to join Bill Longley. We had agreed on a meeting with some of the others, and had gone but a short distance when Bob Lee came up to us with Matt Kirby.

There was news. Barlow had been riding again, and in the north. A farmhouse near Linden had been looted and burned and the stock driven off, but then there was an exchange of shots with some farmers who banded together and Barlow retreated, unwilling to fight when there was loot to be had without fighting. And the troops when called out had found nothing.

Three men had ridden up to Lacy Petraine's house and had ridden around drunk and yelling, but when they tried to force a way in a man suddenly appeared around the corner of the house and spoke to them. Turning to look two of them died in a blast of gunfire, and the third was carried away, seriously wounded.

"And you know who it was? John Tower is working for the widow."

Three men downed in the dark, and two of them killed outright. It was a good shooting. And by John Tower.

He was a man to remember.

While they talked that over I walked away from them. Back

in the field out of sight I waited until a frog croaked and then drew. The heavy Colt snaked out in a swift, fluid motion and was there in my hand, hammer eared back and ready to shoot. Lowering the hammer I tried it again. Yes, I was fast. Was I fast enough?

Gloomily, I strolled back to where they sat under the trees within a step or two of the road. What were we doing here, hiding in the brush like animals? Weary, unwashed and beat, rarely a chance to sleep in a bed, rarely a well-cooked meal like today. They were always telling the foolish romantic stories of outlaws and men on the run . . . the writers of such stories should try it some time; they should try living in swamps, living with sweat, dirt and death.

"I believe," I told them, "that Chance Thorne is getting information to Barlow."

"Who would believe you?" Bob Lee asked. "They were saying today that you were raiding fifty miles south of here."

"Then we'll go into town and show them we're here, and raiding nowhere. We'll make liars of them."

Colonel Amon Belser was the first man we saw. "They say I am out raiding," I told him. "You see me here, and an unlathered horse."

Belser was stiff with anger, for he knew the townspeople were watching, secretly amused. They did not like me, but I was one of their own, and they liked him even less.

"I shall live to see you hang, Cullen Baker!" Belser said. My being here in town made him furious. It was a challenge to the authority he was proud of. "I shall be the first to put a hand on the rope!"

He might be, at that. These days in my dark moods I'd have bet no man that I'd not stretch rope before it was over, only the ones who took me for the hanging would leave some dead behind.

"Colonel," I put both hands on the pommel of my saddle. There were a dozen townsfolk within the sound of my voice, and I wanted them to hear. "Colonel," I said, "if you are in this county or any county that borders it one week from today you'll get what you deserve. It's time we ran all you carpetbaggin' rascals out of here."

"Now see here!" Belser protested. "I—"

"You heard me, Colonel. One week."

He stood there, his face white and he was a mighty worried man. "You'll come to nothing, Cullen Baker," he said. "The very people who think you a hero now will be hunting you down as soon as we are gone."

And when we rode out of town I knew what he had said was true. Folks had never liked me here, and they did not like me now, although because they thought of me as resisting the carpetbaggers they were making me a talked-of man, but once it was over . . . well, they'd be the same then, and they'd start remembering that I'd been a tough lad to deal with.

With the word I'd given Belser I could expect an all-out hunt for me, and no matter what I did I was going to need money. Living in the swamps I'd needed little. A man could hunt himself a living out there, and the boys who had many friends were always coming back with supplies, but the money I'd brought home with me was about gone. Now, if ever, was the time to go after those wild cattle.

It would serve another purpose, too. They would be searching the swamps for me and I'd be down in the Thickets. But I must tell nobody my plans until the last minute.

It was hot and still in the Thickets. In a week of desperately hard work we had rounded up but three hundred head of wild cattle. They were big and mean, most of them, and we'd had our troubles. A man doesn't know how he can sweat until he starts working cattle in the brush. Sometimes for days there wouldn't be a breath of wind, and they grow horseflies down there half as big as sparrows. We worked like dogs, nothing less, and now we had three hundred head together and we were talking it over.

"Barlow's holding about two hundred head of stolen cattle," Longley suggested. "We could go take them from him."

That Longley. He was already ready for trouble. And he was a salty youngster, too.

"We'll take them, Bill," I told him, "but that money won't be ours. Some of the folks that lost those cattle will be wanting the money."

"I wasn't thinking about the money or the cattle," Longley said. "I was thinking about taking them away from Barlow."

"Matt," I asked Kirby, "do you know Lost River?"

"Ought to, I fished along it as a youngster."

"Awhile back," I said, "a fellow was making talk one night and he said there were a lot of wild cattle down there, and that almost nobody lives down there now."

Kirby thought that over. "Well, there's a lot of big meadows down there, always ran to rich grass, and that's mesquite country. I'd say it was top country for cows. But I ain't been there since I was a boy."

We had word from the north. Belser and Chance Thorne were working the swamps along the Sulphur like they had never worked them before. Joel Reese was guiding them, but so far they'd found nothing but a couple of abandoned camps, unused for months. And not ours, either. But what bothered me was word they had been watching the home of Katy Thorne.

One other thing we learned. Two men had come with a horse for the wounded man and had taken him away. She was not molested.

We went back to work on the cattle around Lost River. It was rough country, but a mighty handsome land, too. We had better luck there.

The first white men to come into Texas before the colonies' fight for independence had found wild cattle in the thickets and along the river, most of them descended from cattle left behind by Spanish travelers in the area. Later, cattle had escaped from ranches and fled to the brush, and during the War between the States thousands of cattle had gone unbranded and had run wild to join the herds already there.

Within the thickets there was grass, water and leaves for additional feed. The cattle had worn their own trails through the brush and had become wild animals, and some of them were as fierce as anything that walked, and incredibly huge. Why, down in those thickets I've seen many an old mossyhorn that stood seventeen hands and had a spread of horns better than six feet. Some have been found that I've heard tell of that were ten or eleven feet across.

Kirby knew many of these trails, and I'd scouted around the thickets some on my own. Working that Lost River country we rounded up three hundred head of cattle the first week, and with six hundred head we started north. We had us a big corral spotted.

This corral was in the brush itself, and had been made long since by some Mexicans who had interwoven the surrounding brush into a solid fence strong enough to hold an elephant. We drove our herd north and into that corral. There was water there, and grass enough for a while.

We were on the edge of the Big Thicket now, and we knew exactly where we were going. We entered the Thicket again at a place where a big old cypress leaned above a stream, and we took a dim path, used by game and wild cattle. We rode single file with brush snagging at us on both sides, and we rode armed and ready. This here was going to be war, and believe me, we were ready for it.

The air was stifling. A rabbit started almost from under the feet of the horse I was riding and several times we heard wild hogs grunting in the brush, but we didn't see any. Right then I wasn't wanting to meet a cross old boar right in that narrow trail—a wild boar can be a mean customer at close quarters.

We made a fireless camp that night in a small glade, and we

didn't talk above a whisper. There was a hint of approaching thunderstorm in the air, and we spent the night cleaning guns and getting set. Sam Barlow had asked for trouble when he came north and now we were taking it to him.

My Spencer and two Colts were my weapons, aside from a twelve-inch bowie knife I always carried. For the time and the job it wasn't much to carry. Some of the Barlow men carried five and six pistols, for a cap-and-ball pistol can be a problem to reload, and a man needed fire power.

When I was with the Quantrill crowd that time for a few days I saw many men who carried several pistols stuck into their waistbands, in holsters and on their horses. That young horse thief called Dingus who was with Weaver when I rode away from them had carried four or five pistols. He had red-rimmed eyes and nervous affliction that kept him batting his eyes like an owl in a hailstorm. Nowadays they are talking of him as an outlaw. His rightful name is Jesse James.

It was past noon when we mounted up. The men we were hunting would have eaten and it was siesta time. When we got close to their camp I drew rein.

"We ride in shooting," I said.

Somewhere in the brush ahead of us a woman screamed and a man laughed loudly. Somebody else swore at them to be quiet.

We could see a corral filled with horses and there were a couple of cookfires going, and men lazing about in the shade. Mostly they were watching one man in the center of the group who had a young girl by the arm and a whip in his other hand. "Try gittin' away from me, will you? I'll give you a whuppin' to remember me by. Nothin' like a well-whupped woman, I al-ways says."

There were nearer thirty men present than the fourteen our scout had led us to expect, but several of the horses were damp from hard riding so a party must have just arrived.

"Quite a passel of them, Cullen," Longley commented casually, "but we wanted 'em, didn't we?"

"One shot each," I said, "and then we go in. Make the first one pay." It was at least fifty yards from where we peered through the leaves to the opening into the clearing. "Looks like this will be all the Barlow men we get this time, so don't waste any."

Touching my heel to the horse I started him walking. It was very still except for the laughter from the clearing and the bullying talk of the man with the whip. From each hoof-fall a tiny puff of dust lifted.

It was very hot. Sweat trickled down my cheek and I dried a palm on my jeans. Somewhere off over the thicket a crow called, cawing into the still afternoon. Saddles creaked, and we swung into line opposite the opening, and we were a mere handful to the men inside, but we had wanted a fight, and there was such a thing as surprise. As we swung into line we were within view of at least a third of the men in the clearing, but they were intent upon the struggle between the man and the girl.

Raising my pistol I dropped it dead center on the chest of the man with the whip just as he drew it back for a blow. "All right," I said conversationally, and shot him.

The sharp *bang* of sound was lost in the crashing volley that followed.

The man with the whip dropped the girl's arm and fell on his face in the dust. A man quicker of apprehension than the others rose up sharply from under the trees and dropped in his tracks in the volley that cut him down and several others, and then we went into the clearing at a dead run and swung into two ranks of four each and circled the clearing, shooting.

Men broke and ran in every direction. One who grabbed a shotgun took a bullet in the teeth and fell. Longley leaned from his saddle and grabbed a burning branch which he hurled into the roof of the nearest brush shelter and it went up in a puff of roaring flame.

We scattered out, firing at every target we could see, but the clearing had emptied as though spilled over the edge.

Bob Lee caught up the girl who had been about to be whipped and swung her to his saddle and went out of the camp. Matt Kirby tore open the gate of the corral and stampeded the horses. A shot came from the edge of the clearing and three bullets smashed back a reply, and a man walked from the brush and fell on his face to roll over and stare up at the sun.

And then we were gone, and running. Behind us the Barlow camp was a shambles. The place was a mass of roaring flame, and what cattle and horses they had we drove ahead of us down the trail. Surprisingly, another woman ran from the brush and called out for help. Held prisoner, she had seen her chance, and Bickerstaff held one of the horses for her and she swung aboard with a manner that showed she was not new at riding bareback.

By nightfall we were out of the thicket and headed toward the Louisiana state line. The girl pointed out three cows and a horse that had belonged to her father and we cut them out and gave them to her. Once started we swung up a creek and then went up a road and headed for Fort Worth and the corral enroute where we had left the rest of our cattle.

The girl with her horse and three cows had started home, but she turned back. She had straight, proud eyes and a good, honest way of looking at a man. "Who shall I thank the Good Lord for?" she asked.

"This here is Bob Lee," I said, "and I'm Cullen Baker." Then I named off the others, and she looked at each of them in turn.

"Folks say Cullen Baker is worse than Sam Barlow."

"Don't you believe it," Bill Longley said. "Cullen's honest, but he's driven. The carpetbaggers give us no rest," he added, "and it was Cullen who brought us down here to teach Barlow to stay south of Caddo Lake."

"Thank you," she said, "it's most fittin', what you done. I shall tell folks that it was you saved me."

"You get along home," I said, "or make a new one if yours is gone. This trouble will pass," I added.

We rode to Fort Worth and some of our stock we sold along the way. But most of it we sold in Fort Worth itself.

Several days it had taken us, but we rode careful and stayed shy of the traveled roads, but we traveled less fast than the news of what we had done. In Fort Worth there was already talk of it, and folks were telling that Cullen Baker with fifty men had wiped out a camp of Barlow men. And most folks were pleased.

Actually, there were but eight of us charged the Barlows, and nary a man drew a scratch. We'd been less than three minutes inside that clearing and the surprise had been complete. It was the first time anybody had attacked a Barlow camp—or even found one.

Nor did we wipe them out. Near as we could figure no more than seven were sure enough killed, but we must have wounded that many more. They lost a lot of supplies, clothing, blankets and weapons as well as what stock we drove off.

"Must be a thousand people in Fort Worth," Buck Tinney claimed. He was astonished, a body could see that. Buck, he had never seen a big town before.

"There's bigger towns," his brother Joe said. "New Orleans now, she's bigger. So's Natchez, I reckon."

"Don't seem possible," Buck replied.

We hired us rooms, and bought baths, shaves and haircuts. Comin' into town we looked a likely bunch of curly wolves, but when we got ourselves fixed up we all shaped up like a bunch of dudes.

The fort on the bluff was inside a picket fence, but the building had been abandoned. The log structure that had been the commissary had been taken over by civilians, and the buildings around it had been surrounded by more than a hundred small camps, tents and wagons. There was a black-smith shop, supply store, saloon, a livery stable and various other businesses. Several dozen wagons loaded with bales of cotton were drawn up in the courthouse square.

We stopped on the corner by Haven's hardware store and looked around. The Tinney boys watched the crowd with excited eyes, while Bill Longley went over to the window of Bateman's grocery, nearby.

"Come sundown we meet at the hotel," I suggested. "If things look good we'll stay over, otherwise we light a shuck."

There was something vaguely familiar about a man across the square and it worried me. We wanted to see nobody we knew, although with herds of cattle coming in or passing through any of us might be seen. There were more around who knew Bob Lee and the others than knew me, but they'd be apt to make a connection if they recognized any one of us.

So when we scattered out Bob Lee went across the street with me for a drink. "I could use a decent meal and some clothes," I said to Bob Lee.

My clothes looked miserable and I'd been thinking of that. The cattle paid off in good money and I was feeling it. Also, good clothes would be a sort of disguise, for nobody had ever seen me in any, leastways not around here.

"Ever think of going West?" I asked it suddenly, so it surprised even me.

"My family are here," Bob Lee said, after a minute, "and we've a difficulty with the Peacock family. No telling when it will end. Yes, I've thought of it, or maybe Mexico."

"I was thinking about it."

"You've nobody here."

"Nothing but a tough reputation."

"Is that why you wanted this drive? To get money to go West?"

He never got an answer to that one because right then I lifted my glass and looked down the bar into the eyes of John Tower.

My left side was toward the bar and my left-hand gun was under the edge of the bar and out of easy grasp. It was my right hand held the drink.

Tower started along the bar toward us, and Lee caught my expression, knowing there was trouble. "Stand easy," I whispered, "it's the man rides for Lacy Petraine."

"Who used to ride for Belser."

Tower was carefully dressed in a black broadcloth suit, and was clean-shaven but for his mustache. "Having yourselves a blowout?" he asked.

"Looking around," I said. "We may open a ready-to-wear."

Bill Longley had come in. "Or a funeral parlor," he said. "Could be a lot of business in that line."

John Tower glanced at Longley. "I might contribute a little, myself. But don't start business my way. I'm not a trouble-hunting man."

"Neither are we," I said.

"There's a story around town that somebody named Cullen Baker cleaned up Barlow's guerrillas, and you would be surprised how much friendly talk it started about Cullen Baker. A few more operations like that and he could run for governor."

He put down his glass. "By the way, Mrs. Petraine is in town, and she'd like to talk to you."

"Later," I said.

Matt Kirby came up the street with the Tinney boys. "Dud Butler's in town," he whispered, "and four or five with him."

Butler I remembered. It had been him I'd seen across the street. He had been one of the boys with Chance the first time they set on me, but lately he'd been reported riding with Sam Barlow. A big, dirty, oafish boy, he had grown into a man of the same sort.

"It's my fight," I said.

"He knows me," Bob Lee said. "He rides with that Peacock outfit."

In a tailor shop we got ourselves fitted into black broadcloth suits, and Tower came in. "You would do well to talk to Mrs. Petraine," he said. "She particularly requested you come to see her."

"Watch yourself," Longley advised. "It might be a trap."

"I don't need a trap," Tower replied. "I skin my own cats."

Lacy Petraine was in a small place on a street off the square where an elderly widow and her maiden lady sister served meals to the better class of traveler.

She was seated alone and for an instant she did not recognize me in the new suit. "You are quite the gentleman, Mr. Baker. You should wear such clothes all the time."

"You wanted to see me?"

"I wanted to buy your land—all of it."

So I sat down and put my hat on the chair beside me. All my memories of anything were here in Texas, and my folks had left their mark upon the house and upon the land. Pa was always a-tinkering at things, and he built every inch of fence on the place with my help, and some of it we had cleared together of brush and trees.

"It isn't for sale," I said.

"Cullen," she leaned across the table toward me, and she was wearing some fancy perfume like nothing I'd ever smelled before, "I know how you feel, but there's nothing here for you any more. I know how you feel because we are much alike in many ways, but your only hope is to leave."

There was truth in that, more truth than I cared to admit, even though I was more than half-convinced already. The carpetbaggers would go, but Chance Thorne would stay, and he would have a glib story to tell, and with his family background, he'd be apt to make it stick. Meanwhile, who was to speak for me?

Would Bob Lee be left? Or Bickerstaff, or any of the others?

"Believe me, Cullen, you are facing a fight you cannot win. I tried to win it once, and then tried again and again, but my reputation followed me. But you could ride away into the West where you used to be, and nobody would be the wiser."

"Maybe, maybe you're right."

"You've frightened them, Cullen, and they're out to get you now, and believe me, they don't dare let you live."

Finishing my coffee I put money on the table and got up. Suddenly I felt cramped for space. "Not now," I said, "but thanks for the offer."

"Don't wait too long," she warned.

Turning away from the table I glanced out the window at the street. With Dud Butler out there Bob Lee was in danger, too. He should not be away from the others.

"Cullen," Lacy spoke very low, "if you're thinking of Katy Thorne it won't do. She's to be married."

My back was to her and I was glad. Katy to be married? That was impossible. She would have said something, she would have . . . but why should she?

"I had not heard."

"It has been developing a long time, Cullen, even before you returned, and I am surprised you had not heard of it."

"Who is he?"

"Tom Warren, the schoolteacher. He began courting her over a year ago, and I believe his family have some distant connection with Katy's Aunt Florence."

She came up behind me where I stood looking into the street. "Don't sell me the land, Cullen, but go, please go."

"Why are you so concerned?"

The question stopped her, and I could see she didn't even know herself, and looking at her I knew I'd never seen a woman so beautiful, and somehow I had a sudden feeling if I was to reach out and take her in my arms that she wouldn't resist, not even a mite. And we were all alone in here, at this hour.

"I must go," I said, feeling a fool to have such ideas. What could she want with me?

Lacy put her hand on my arm. "Come and see me, Cullen. Please do."

"Why, sure. Sure, Lacy, I'll come."

My gun was thrust behind my belt under the edge of the coat I was wearing, and when I stepped out I looked one way and the other, but saw nobody.

The square was filled with wagons and as it was growing late in the afternoon folks were moving slower and the square was quieter. Yet suddenly the urge was on me to get out of town, to ride, to get away. I needed a campfire and time to think. There was no reason why I should be so wrought up about Katy marrying. What could she mean to me?

My eyes were busy and I figured I was seeing everything, that I'd scanned every wagon, every doorway, every spot a man could hide, yet suddenly the voice came from behind me and it was Dud Butler.

"I'm a-gonna kill you, Cullen!"

All movement stopped and I knew without turning that his gun was ready to kill me as I turned. Only I was already turning.

There was no thinking, no thought and response, just that challenge and the months of training I'd given myself and before he was through talking I was shooting.

The report of that Dragoon Colt cut a hard line across the silence of the square.

Dud lifted on his tiptoes, took one teetering step forward and fell flat, and he was dead before he touched the ground.

Dud had never known anything but a flash of flame and a stunning blow over the heart.

From nowhere they closed around me, guns drawn, facing outward. Lee, Longley and the Tinney boys, with Kirby coming up, leading all our horses. And by a cotton wagon was Jack

English and he was holding a Spencer, and beyond him Bickerstaff facing the other way with a Henry .44.

A tall man with a gray mustache stepped over and stared down at Dud Butler's body, then he looked around at me. "I say it was a fair shootin'," he said positively, "but I never did see a man shuck a gun so quick."

The crowd was gathering, and one man stared hard at me and said, "He called a name, sounded like Cullen."

"He's no Cullen," Longley grinned at the man, "this here's our boss, he's a cattleman from the Gulf shore."

Matt Kirby reined his horse over to look down at Butler's body. "Why, this man looks like one of the Barlow crowd! I'd swear that's Dud Butler!"

We mounted up. After Kirby's comment it was not likely anybody would come forward and admit to being a friend of Butler, and therefore likely to be taken for one of the Barlow outlaws.

Riding swiftly out of town we took the trail west until we hit a cattle trail that would partly cover our tracks, and then we swung south and east, keeping to low ground so's not to be seen more than we could help. We expected no pursuit but operated on the idea that a man can't be too careful.

We camped by a small stream that flowed into the Trinity after riding several miles in the water to leave no more trail than we had to. It was past midnight when we bedded down, and when Longley was pulling off his boots he said, "That old feller back there was right. I never did see a man get a gun out so fast."

On the bluff across the river a lone coyote yapped a shrill challenge at the moon, and a faint breeze rustled the cottonwood leaves.

Taking my pipe out of my pocket I lighted up, feeling mighty solemn. Bob Lee was rolling a cigarette, a trick he had learned from Mexicans. "Could be you're right, Cullen," he said. "Maybe we should all go West."

FIVE

When I crawled out from under my blankets in the cold
dawn I had an urge to cut and run. Prodding the gray
coals with a stick I found a little fire and threw on some leaves
and then some branches.

Why was I going back, anyway? I was away from there with a
good start on the road west and I was a complete fool to go
back and make a target of myself.

A stranger had camped with us, a man who came in late and
wanted to bed down, and although none of us knew him there
was no way we could shut him out. He was as full of news as a
dry farm widow, and told us there was a regiment of soldiers
moved to Marshall, and rumor had it that a company was to be
located in Jefferson, and another in Clarksville. Nor were these
raw, unseasoned troops we'd had around that neck of the
woods, but tough veterans of the recent war, and real fighting
men. Chance Thorne, this stranger said, had been searching
the swamps with a bunch of Union Leaguers hunting for that
there Cullen Baker.

When I had water on the fire for coffee I made up my mind. I was riding to Blackthorne.

Kirby caught me shaving and had to speak up. "A feller shaves he mostly goes courtin'."

"Business," I told them, "although I'm stopping at Blackthorne."

"They'll be ready for you, Cull." Kirby paused. "Want me to show some place? We're about of a size and build and color of hair. I've heard it said we favor, from behind, anyway. I could draw them off."

"No use getting shot for me. I'll manage."

"We'll be at the Elbow," Bob Lee suggested. "Come there."

It was a wearing thing, being geared for trouble at any minute when all I wanted was a little peace. Stuffing my gear in my saddlebags I considered that, realizing I was a hunted man drawing nearer to the hunters.

It was late when I rode up through the orchard to Blackthorne. I'd switched to the mule and I tied him in the old stable under the wisteria vine, but there was a horse tied outside the house and I felt irritation. I'd hoped to find Katy alone.

A glance through the window showed a young man, well-dressed, and a stranger to me. From the description I knew it must be Thomas Warren, that schoolteacher Lacy told me was to marry Katy. Right then I was a jealous man, and no reason for it; I'd no claim on her.

Aunt Flo had a quick warmth in her welcome that pleased me, not knowing how anybody would feel about me here, and Katy's smile was quick and excited. "Cullen! You were the last person we expected! We heard the Army was searching for you."

Katy turned quickly. "Cullen, this is Thomas Warren, he teaches school near here."

"A pleasure," I said, and held out my hand. Warren wore a gun, probably a Patterson Colt, but carried it in his pocket. He ignored my hand.

100

"I cannot say the same. If you have friendship for Miss Thorne you will leave at once."

"Why, Tom!" Katy was surprised. "Cullen is a friend of mine, and a very good friend."

"That surprises me," Warren replied stiffly. "I cannot understand how a lady of quality can endure the presence of this . . . this. . . ."

Ignoring him, I said to her, "It's good to see you, Katy. Very good to see you."

It was a fine sort of thing to see her pleasure in my new clothes. In the dark suit I knew I looked well, but anything would have looked better than the clothes I'd been wearing.

"You look every inch the Southern gentleman," Katy said. "Have you eaten?"

"Camp fare by a man who is no cook."

Aunt Flo, to whom a hungry man was a delight, and reason for much bustling in the kitchen, was busy right off. Warren stood there at one side looking furious. Anybody else but him and anywhere else but this I'd have read to him from the Book for talking like he had, but this was Katy's house and I was her guest . . . and he, this Warren, was to marry her.

"Have you thought," Warren interrupted, "what would happen if the soldiers should come?"

Katy turned on him. "Cullen Baker was welcome in this house when Uncle Will lived here, and will always be welcome. I am sorry, Tom, that you disapprove, but if you do not mind being in the same house with Cullen Baker, we would like to have you stay."

His face paled, and for an instant I figured he would leave, then he sat down abruptly.

Katy asked about Fort Worth, so she had heard about Dud Butler. "I wasn't surprised," she said quietly. "He was always a cruel, trouble-making boy."

Warren glanced at her, shocked.

101

"Mr. Warren," Katy explained, "comes from New England. I believe he finds us somewhat barbaric."

"Not you!" Warren replied hastily. "Not you at all!"

"This is still a frontier," I said, "and there was a time when they carried guns to church even in New England."

"It was not the same. There were Indians."

"There are many kinds of savages."

"I scarcely believe there is basis for comparison." Warren was brusque. "Fighting off red Indians is very different from killing white men in the street."

"One time Will Thorne told me about the Puritans wanting to go down to Baltimore and burn out some folks just because they liked music, parties and dancing. That seems mighty savage to me."

Warren stood up. "I believe I must go," he said. "I did not realize you expected company."

When Warren was gone we sat silent, and I did not know what to say, or how to begin. If she was to marry this man it was her affair, but it was wrong; he was no man for her. And it was not only that he had not liked me, but there seemed something wrong about him, the feeling one has sometimes about a bad horse, yet what could be wrong about a school-teacher? Maybe it was that he was too sure he was right, he was almost, it appeared to me, a fanatic, and fanatics are dangerous men.

Yet why should I mind? She had been kind to me when there had been no one else. Turning my head to watch the candlelight reflected on her face I thought suddenly something I had not thought before—I loved her.

How does a man like me know what love is? There was nothing much in my life to tell me, but there was a feeling I felt for her that I had never felt before, for anyone.

"Your corn is tall," Katy said suddenly. "It is ready to harvest."

"I'm leaving Texas," I said.

"You're actually going?"

"Yes."

"When, Cullen? When?"

"Soon—in the next few days."

"Cullen, I— You've no idea how I've hoped for this!"

"You want to be rid of me?"

She put her hand on mine. "You know it isn't that. You simply haven't a chance here, and somewhere else you can make a fresh start, and you'll have a chance to live a decent life."

"Everything I have is here." I said it sullenly. "If I leave here there is nothing for me."

"There is everything for you, Cullen. You are young, strong, and you have intelligence. You can do anything you wish to do, if you wish it enough."

Looking at her I thought that there was one thing I could never have, no matter how much I wanted it. Anger stirred me and I got up, anger at myself and at the place life had given me. But she was right, and there was nothing here for me and the sooner I left the better.

"I must go."

"Wait." Katy blew out the candle and we opened the door and stepped out into the darkness. There was a faint breeze from over the swamp bringing a breath of ancient earth and rotting wood and dead leaves, the heavy scent of blossoms, too, and the coolness of still waters, those shaded waters where soon I would go no more.

Suddenly the anger welled up in me again and I knew that no matter who she was to marry I must say what there was in me to say. "Katy," I said, "would you—"

They stepped out of the darkness so quietly that I had no time to think or to act. There were a dozen of them with rifles leveled, and in the faint moonlight they were clearly visible. And my only thought was that if I made a move now Katy might be injured.

"Do not move, Cullen. This time we have you." The voice was the voice of Chance Thorne.

He stepped through the line of armed men and stood there in the moonlight, tall, straight and handsome. "And now, Cullen Baker, you'll hang."

A man came from behind me and took my two Colts. Katy remained beside me and, looking up at me, she whispered, "What was it, Cullen? What did you start to ask me?"

"A foolish thing," I said, "and nothing at all, really. Nothing at all."

How could a man who was to be hung ask such a question? And Chance Thorne would not let me escape again, and if I was not to be surprised, they would hang me before we ever reached Jefferson.

"Go inside, Katy," Chance said. "If anything is to happen I do not want you to see it."

"I'll stay." From behind the house Bert appeared. He was a former slave who had returned a few days before when he could find no work. "Bert, get my horse, will you?"

"I'll not permit that." Chance spoke angrily. "There might be shooting."

Katy smiled at him. "That is why I shall go along, so there will be no shooting. I want to be sure this prisoner really gets to prison."

Chance hesitated, not knowing how to stop her. I knew he intended to hang me, and realized that only Katy stood between the hangman's rope and me.

Yet I could wait and listen, and maybe there would be a spot of luck between now and the moment of death. At the same time the slightest wrong move would have me ballasted down with lead.

"It's all right," I told Katy. "Nothing will happen."

Joel Reese laughed sardonically. "Don't be too sure of that. I've already got the rope."

There were men here who feared me, and fearing me they

hated me because of their fear, and Katy herself might be in danger if they became too drunk or too reckless to care. Yet any mob is composed of cowards, and each hopes to commit brutality and cruelty within the safety of the mob. He does not wish to be singled out.

So I chuckled, and never did I feel less like it, but I knew whatever must be done must be done now, while they were still sober-headed enough to listen and to know fear. "You have the rope, Joel, but have you eyes that see in the dark? Eyes that can see an aimed rifle before it hits home?"

Oh, I had their attention now, and I meant to push home the point. If I reached Jefferson or Boston or wherever they meant to take me, I would be a surprised man. Yet much as they wished to hang me they wanted to live even more.

"Did you believe I was alone here? The boys are out there now, just beyond the edge of darkness, and they're watching. If anything happens to me not one of you will live."

"You're lyin'!" Reese yelled at me. "You're lyin', damn you!" But there was a note in his voice that sounded from the fear in his belly.

We rode out, and I was tied to my mule which Reese had found, and my feet tied to the stirrups. There was a man on either side of me, three before and three behind, and others scattered about, and each man rode with a gun ready in his hands.

The words I had spoken as a warning had touched them to the quick. Once, when out in the forest a twig snapped, they jumped in their saddles, lifting their rifles.

"No use to fight," I told them. "When they want you they'll take you. Right now you are alive because they have seen that I am unhurt. If anything happens to me not one man jack of you will live to see town."

"Shut up!" Reese said angrily. "When we get you into town it will be a different story."

The stocky man on his right leaned toward him. "I want a

hand on the rope that hangs you, Baker! That there rope will sell for a pretty penny. Feller could cut it into three- or four-inch lengths and sell them as the rope that hung Cullen Baker! I could stay drunk for a month on what I'd make from that!"

Out in the dark forest an owl hooted, only suddenly I knew all my talk had not been empty talk, for that owl hoot was Bill Longley! From the road ahead I heard it again, only that time it wasn't Longley who hooted, but one of the others.

A moment later the sound was repeated from behind and on both sides.

Reese swore savagely, but the fright in his voice was plain to hear. The riders behind began to bunch up as if afraid of being caught alone.

"You'd be better off turning me loose," I said. "If I should fall off my horse there'd be a lot of dead men around."

There was no chance to rescue for my own crowd were outnumbered three to one, and I'd probably be killed in the fight. So bunched tightly we rode on into town, and the jail was opened for me.

Chance came to the cell door. "So now we'll see the end of you, Cullen, and we'll get the rest of them, too."

"Not a chance."

"We've drawn them close now, so we'll just bring in the soldiers from the other towns and draw a tight line around outside of them. Then we'll just move in toward town and bring them all right on in."

When I said nothing to that, Chance added, "We've informers. Bob Lee won't last any longer than his next visit home, and Longley will go with him."

"You had a bit of luck catching me," I told him, "you won't be so lucky with them."

He laughed. "We had word you were there, although not from a regular informer."

From the window I could overlook about an acre of grass-covered lot and could look diagonally up the street. Judge Tom Blaine's office was in view: he was an old friend of Katy's.

It was warm and still. Nothing moved outside in the night. From a few windows along the street, light fell into the black avenue, and overhead wind rustled in the leaves of the elms along the walk. Occasionally someone walked up the street and their heels echoed on the boards of the walk. Off across the town a dog barked.

Reaching up I took hold of the window bars and tried them with my hands. No man I'd ever met but one German in the mines of Colorado had been able to lift as much as I, or pull as much. Taking hold of the bars I tested them with my strength, for although set in stone such bars are often loose.

They held firm, and I tried a little harder, and nothing happened. Well, that was a remote chance, anyway. Prowling the square cell, which was about ten by ten, I tried to find some weakness, some way in which I could get out. The door into the space beyond the bars seemed the best chance, but I dared not try that with a guard in the outer office. It looked like the barred door might be set only in the wooden frame, and if that was true I'd have it out of there, door and all.

Somebody had informed. Who? Katy? That was impossible. What about that schoolteacher, Warren? But he had talked so much about Katy getting hurt if the soldiers came, and it was unlikely. He had no real reason.

Some time after that I fell asleep, and I opened my eyes with a rooster crowing next door, and I sat up.

One thing I had . . . the derringer.

When they had taken my Colts and rifle they had looked only so far as the bowie knife, and no farther. But in this country derringers were relatively unknown, and they were considered a woman's gun. There was nothing very feminine about those two .44 slugs.

The man who brought me food was a stranger wearing a blue uniform coat. He was tall, stooped and gawky. His big Adam's apple bobbed as he looked at me. "You that there Cullen Baker?"

"I'm Baker."

"They fixin' to hang you."

"When?"

"Maybe tomorry. I dunno." The guard eyed me thoughtfully. "You married."

"I'm not so lucky," I said. "Only two things I'll leave behind are a mule and a corn crop."

He looked at me and blinked his eyes. "A corn crop? They said you was an outlaw."

"First crop I ever raised all to myself. I used to help my pa, but he died while I was out West. It's a good crop, only I couldn't do all I wanted, hiding in the swamps and all."

"What about the mule?"

"He's a buckskin riding mule with an ingrown disposition. Ornery most of the time, but once started he'll take you from here to yonder with less water and less food in more heat than any horse you ever saw."

"I got me a team of mules in Pike County."

From the front of the jail a voice raised. "Hey, Wesley!"

The food he brought me was not bad. Side meat, eggs and hominy grits, so I ate it, thinking of the night. The coffee was strong enough to float a bullet.

I'd not see that corn crop again. It was like my other dreams and would come to nothing, but one thing I did know, some way, somehow, I was not going to hang. The more I looked at that door the more I liked it, and the warmer I felt toward the slipshod carpenter who'd put it up. It did not look like it was bolted to the stones and if it was just fitted I could take it out of there like you'd take a picture out of a frame.

Wesley brought in a newspaper. It was a week old but it had things to say of me. They were calling me "the swamp fox of the Sulphur" and they were calling it a "new rebellion" and writing wild stories of all I was supposed to have done.

Standing at the window I saw Seth Rames out there. Seth was a hard man, and a close friend to Bob Lee. He had been through some fighting in that country, but he was not a known man in Jefferson. They knew him over west of here, and in Louisiana, but not right about here. He was standing on the street lighting his pipe.

Nobody needed to tell me why he was there. Seth Rames was a tough man and he was no Reconstruction man, but dead set against them with at least one soldier killing held against him. If Seth was here it was because he was a friend to my friends, and was a man not known in Jefferson. So they were thinking about me, and they were planning. But I almost wished them away from there. I wanted no man in trouble because of me.

While I was still figuring what Seth Rames might be doing out there, there was a footstep outside the cell door and I turned around to see John Tower standing there.

He glanced back toward the cubbyhole of an office that was in front of the jail. Then he said quietly, "Lacy was afraid of this."

"She warned me."

"She also," he spoke very low, "wants you out. And she'll still buy your land."

"Is that what she wants to get me out?"

John Tower's lips tightened and there was not much that was pleasant in the way he looked at me. "She's not that kind," he said, and his voice was mighty cold. "She wants you out, that's all."

"We won't have any argument there."

"Have you any ideas?"

Considering that, I decided I had none. All I knew was that somehow I was going to get out of here, but the walls were stone and they were thick and there was a guard around most of the time. The door frame was of two-by-sixes and they were fitted into the stone door in a mighty snug fashion, with the barred door hung on this frame. A man might take that frame out of there if he had time and there was no one around to hear. It would be a big job, but I was figured to be a mighty powerful man and might do it. But I didn't want my life to rest on that, but as a last resort I'd sure enough have a try at it.

At noon Katy Thorne came to see me. Her face was pale and her eyes looked larger than I'd ever seen them. She was frightened, I could see that.

"Now see here," I said, "what's worrying you?"

"You ask that? Oh, Cullen! I've been afraid of this, so afraid!"

Well, I looked down at my hands on those bars and then at her. Maybe I should have kept my mouth shut, her going to marry him and all, but I'm no kind of a hero and a bad lot generally, and the way I figured it there was only one answer.

"Chance told me somebody tipped them off. And it was right after Warren left your place."

"Cullen!" she exclaimed. "You can't believe that! Oh, but that's absurd!"

"Who else then?"

That stopped her, and she stared back at me, as if thinking something out, then she said, "Maybe Judge Tom could stop this."

"The hanging you mean?" At her surprised expression, I added, "I know all about it."

We were quiet for a few minutes and then in a low voice I whispered to her to get hold of the boys, at all costs, and to warn them to stay away from Jefferson and me, that I was being used as bait for the lot of them. They were going to hang me, they'd said that, but one thing worried me. How were they going to do it? Now all they had to do was hang me, all right, but without a trial and all folks might start asking why, and some of those Reconstruction people might ask questions themselves. Some of them were honest, I'd heard.

Right about then I had an idea that I didn't like even a little: Suppose there was a jail delivery by Sam Barlow? No sooner did I have the idea than I was sure that was just how Chance would want it, and no blame could fall on anybody but a fight between outlaws. It was just the sort of thing Barlow would want to do and that Chance would think of.

"Katy, you'd better get out of town. Go back to Blackthorne and stay there. There'll be trouble before this is over, but if you can stop the boys from trying anything I'll be forever grateful."

We talked then as folks will, about much of nothing, but making talk because I didn't want to see her leave, and from the way she acted she wasn't overeager to go.

Whatever happened now must happen here in town, and I could see trouble building around like the thunderheads piling up before a storm.

"Cullen, I'm frightened."

She was, too. Guess it was the first time since I was a youngster that anybody worried about me. Well, right now I was worried about me, too. I'd no idea of hanging to any tree for the pleasure of Chance Thorne and those others. But I didn't see much of a way out.

Sure, I had the derringer. In one way it was less than good to have. It had two bullets. It would be fine if nobody called my bluff, but if I had to shoot with that gun and only two bullets . . . well, it would be an invitation from them to mow me down, and they'd do it.

"You'd best go home, Katy. I'm afraid there'll be trouble here, and if there's careless shooting you might get hurt."

"I'm afraid for you."

Well, I grinned at her, although I wasn't feeling too much like grinning. "Forget it," I said. "There's no use both of us being scared."

When she turned to go she started to say something, but then she stopped and hurried out, and I stood there looking after her and I knew that no matter how she felt, that I was in love with her and had been for some time. Maybe I'd been

111

afraid to admit it to myself, because I'm usually a man who speaks up for what he wants, and I back up for no man in trying to get what I want, but with her it seemed so hopeless that I guess I'd shied off from even admitting to myself that I was in love with her.

When she was gone something inside me exploded. Maybe it was anger: I don't know about that, for a man has many emotions and they are not as easily catalogued as folks would have you believe. Anyway, something happened and I just busted wide open inside, and I was suddenly frantic to get out of there. Not that I was wild or anything. I'm not the sort to go off my head. Inside I was wild but outwardly I was cold as ice, and I really began thinking. Get a man or an animal in a trap and they really do some thinking. There had to be a way out of here, and I meant to go out, but I didn't want to die in the process. There was no difference to me between being hung or shot. I just had a healthy urge to go on living, for no matter how bad it was there was always a chance it could get better, and that I could make it better. Now, with the whole West opening out for me, I wanted out of here.

So I paced the floor. Again I tried the bars on that window— nothing doing. So I went to the door and took hold of the bars of the door and I braced my feet. With all my strength I began to pull, not wanting to be free at the moment, but to test the strength of that door. Nothing stirred, yet somehow I had a feeling there was weakness there.

The floor was solid stone and well fitted together. Circling the walls I could find no weakness there. The door was a slim chance and it meant going out through the front, and if I made too much noise that guard would be in on me, but tonight I was going to try it. Believe me, I was.

So I went back to my cot and laid down. It was almost two in the afternoon, and it was hot.

Wesley came to the door with a fresh bucket of water. He

put it down and handed me a gourd with a handle long enough to reach the bucket through the bars. "He'p yo'self," he said. "A man gits mighty dry."

Maybe I napped for a spell, but it couldn't have been long for the first thing I know Chance Thorne is there at the bars looking in at me. "Sleeping your life away?" he said. "If I had only a few hours to live, I'd be awake and enjoying it."

Well, I got up off that crummy cot and stretched myself, and took my time, looking bored all the while. Not that I was feeling that way. I was wishing I could get through those bars and have a try at him with my hands. "Don't let it bother you. I'll live to spit on your grave."

He didn't like it. Chance wanted me to beg, he wanted me humble, but surprisingly enough, suddenly I felt very good. Maybe it was because no man really believes he's going to die at a time like that. Right up to the last minute he's hoping something will happen to save his bacon. Whatever was going to save mine had better happen pretty sudden.

"Don't think you'll get out," Chance told me, "Bob Lee can't help you. Nobody can. Lee is too busy hunting a hole himself. This town is ringed with soldiers, and others are searching the swamps like they've never been searched. Peacock had men watching for Lee at his home, and you know how any Peacock hates a Lee, and Bob in particular. If he isn't dead within a few hours, he'll die within the next week or two."

Right now I was thinking of tonight and I wanted to feel him out. Turned out it didn't take any careful words to get at the truth, he was too sure of himself, and of me.

"You can't get away with hanging me without a trial," I said. "Folks will be down here investigating right off."

He chuckled, and couldn't resist a good brag. "Not if you're hung by somebody who isn't authorized," he said. "Supposing the soldiers should all hear about Bob Lee being some place and take off after him. No telling what might happen here in town, you've made a lot of enemies, Cullen, enemies like Sam Barlow."

Showed I could guess how he was thinking, anyway. The worst of it was, it could happen just that way.

What happened next I never heard of until later. It was Katy herself told me of it, and Jane Watson told me some more that she'd overheard. Jane was the name of that girl I'd helped take out of Sam Barlow's camp, the one who was about to get whipped.

If anybody was thinking of Jane Watson right then it wasn't me, and I didn't even know her name, to tell the truth. She was one person I'd forgotten all about, and never expected to see again, but the way it turned out she hadn't forgotten me. I like folks, but never expect too much of them. We're all human, and most folks are apt to forget favors you've done them, fact is, they remember the favors they do for you far better. Right then I didn't know it, but Jane had come up to Jefferson with blood in her eye, wanting to do something for me, and later she came to see me at the jail, but first she heard a conversation that was repeated to me.

Seems Thomas Warren, that schoolteacher met Katy in a store. Jane Watson, who knew neither of them at the time, overheard what followed.

Katy was looking at some yard goods when Warren came up to her. "Have you heard the news?"

"News?"

"They've arrested Cullen Baker. They plan to hang him."

"He will be tried first, I think." According to Jane it didn't seem that Katy wanted to discuss it.

"There are rumors that he will be taken out of jail and hung immediately."

"You don't like him, do you?"

"He's a common outlaw, a murderer. How could I like him?"

"You know that I do?"

Warren had shrugged at that remark. "You feel you should like him because he's from here and because your Uncle Will liked him. He will bring you nothing but trouble, and it will ruin your reputation."

"My reputation is my own concern."

"It may," Warren said stiffly, "some day be your husband's concern. That is why I feel concerned."

From what Jane said, Katy looked startled, and she said merely, "You have no reason to feel concerned, Tom. I like you, but the idea of you as my husband, if that is what you mean, why that's impossible."

"Why? Why should it be?"

Katy drew away from him at this point and perfectly composed she said, "Mr. Warren, I am afraid you are assuming an interest on my part that has never existed. As for Cullen, no matter what is said of him, I know him to be a good man."

Warren was excited then, or so Jane told me. He was so excited that it didn't appear just right somehow, or maybe that he was a little off balance. Anyway, he told Katy, "He won't look so nice at the end of a rope! He is an evil man! That's why I—"

"Why you—*what?*"

Abruptly he walked away from her, but at the door he had looked back. "You will feel different when you're rid of him," he said, "and then I'll be back."

Right then, as Warren went out, Lacy Petraine came in, and she walked right up to Katy. "Miss Thorne, we need your help."

And that was when Jane Watson went up to them both and told them why she had come to Jefferson. She knew how they both felt, and she said right out what she had come for.

There was one other thing Chance had said that stuck in my mind, and with good cause. Just as he was leaving he had said that he and Joel Reese and some others would be back before I was hung. They wanted, Chance said, a private session with me in the cell. They would, he promised, make it easy for me to die. They would make me want to die.

And that was enough to give a man something to think about.

SIX

Katy had told me a good bit about Warren, and some of it I could sort of piece together, seeing how he shaped up to me. He'd been born, she said, into a house that was run by two maiden aunts, and what happened to his folks, I never did hear. Only those two aunts must have made much of him as a youngster and, from what he told Katy, they had taught him to study hard, to stay away from rough boys and rough play, and to avoid all the vices named and unnamed in this most wicked of worlds.

A man brought up like that is likely to grow up but not out, and I expect the world he lived in at twenty-seven wasn't much different than it had been at seventeen. To me he seemed like a man mighty positive of his own rightness, and usually those sort are all torn up inside by a lot of petty worries and petty ideas. But with those aunts always telling him he would be somebody.

Maybe like some others he figured when the war was over that Texas was the place to come. A lot of young men had been

117

killed, and there should be a lot of girls around with money. I heard talk of that sort, myself, and I wouldn't be surprised if something like that had been in his mind when he met Katy Thorne.

Right now he was probably mad clear through, but less at Katy than at me.

Standing by the window I saw Katy come out of the store with Lacy Petraine and Jane Watson. Now there was something to think about, and I was hoping that I was the only one doing that kind of thinking. Only I wasn't. Thomas Warren was standing across the street under a tree staring at them.

Why? Well, it sort of didn't fit, if you know what I mean. Three women might get together and talk, that's true, but Lacy wasn't considered a quite nice person and Katy Thorne was as much aristocracy as we had in that corner of Texas right then, and she would have been aristocracy anywhere else, too.

Jane Watson? Well, she came of a poor family on a small place south of here. There was no likely reason for her to be in town, and less reason for her to even know Katy or Lacy. Maybe Warren was thinking what I was, that the only common tie those three had was me, Cullen Baker.

It was hot in that cell with the sun beating against the outer wall. Sometimes I'd hear a rig go by in the street with a jingle of harness or the crack of a whip, or I'd hear people talking, or hear the *clank* of horseshoes from a vacant lot up the street where somebody was always playing.

From the outer office I heard simply nothing at all, so the guard must be sitting outside against the front wall.

There was nobody else in the jail but me, although there were three empty cells. If I could get that door out of the way I would have to go through that little office, overpower one or two guards and then would come out on a street where most of the crowd would be enemies and most of the remaining folks would want to stay out of it. Therefore that derringer was useless unless I could get out when nobody was around.

118

Once outside there would be the problem of slipping past the patrols and getting into the swamps. Chances were an easy thousand to one I'd never make it.

Unless I was altogether wrong, all hell was building up outside. Knowing the boys like I did, I knew no matter what I wanted they would try to get me out of there, just as I would try to help them. This was a fact known to Colonel Belser, too, and to Chance Thorne. It was a good guess they'd leave a hole for them to come through, then trap them inside, maybe right here at the jail.

And if my figuring was right, and from what Chance had said it was right, somewhere to the south Sam Barlow would be riding up to lynch me.

And right here in town three women were in a way to get themselves into a lot of trouble trying to help me. Whatever else happened this here had shown me how many friends I had, and for a man with a bad reputation, I was doing all right.

Only I didn't dare let them help me.

Somehow, some way, I had to get out and away before any of them could do a thing to help, before they could get their tails in a crack trying to help.

To have friends a man has to be friendly, and to get others to think of you, you have to think of others. I wanted no man dying for me, and the mere fact that Seth Rames was in Jefferson showed something was up, and whatever Lacy Petraine was in, John Tower was in, too.

It was closing in toward sundown. If all went as I figured, it would be some time after midnight before Barlow arrived, and right about midnight when I could expect the visit from Chance Thorne and his men.

That meant that some time before midnight I was going to have to be out of here, and the sooner the better. If I was going to help those friends who wanted to help me, I'd have to get out before they could get far enough in to be in real trouble.

Right then was when Jane Watson showed up. Wesley brought her in, blushing up to his freckled ears, and I could see he was mighty taken with her.

When he left she moved right up to the bars. "It will be at ten," she spoke quickly and quietly. "John Tower will hold up the guards and we will be outside in the buckboard. He will have two horses, and when the two of you start to leave, we will drive across the street ahead of anybody who might try to chase you."

It was silly, and I told her so. Same time I knew it was silly enough and simple enough to work. It meant making an outlaw out of John Tower, and I didn't see why he should do that for me. I said as much to Jane.

"It isn't for you, although he likes you. He is in love with Lacy Petraine."

She told me about that, and it added up to something none of us had known. Of course, I had my own bit of knowing about John Tower, but that's neither here nor there. According to what Jane said, John Tower had walked up to Mrs. Petraine and he had told her right out, "Mrs. Petraine, I am the man who shot Terence O'Donnell. I shot your husband, Mrs. Petraine."

Lacy being what she was, I could understand what followed. That was a sight of woman, believe you me.

"Terry," she said, "always believed himself a better man with a gun than he was."

"I am sorry."

"Yes, as he would have been sorry had he killed you. Mr. Tower, let me assure you of this. Terence would have killed you if he could. He was not a man to make foolish gestures with a gun."

"Is that all? I mean now that you know this you will probably want me to leave your employ?"

"That was long ago, Mr. Tower, and in another world than this. We have both changed since then. I believe I was very

120

much in love with Terence, but now it is like a dream, and like all dreams, it has ended."

But from what Jane said it was there between them, and they knew they loved each other, and they both knew that in time something would come of it. So now he was to help me because of her.

Well, now. Maybe down inside I'd figured she would help me because it was me she liked, or because she thought me a fine figure of a man, like she had practically said, one time. Showed how wrong a man could be, and I felt kind of let down and cooled off, if you know what I mean.

Well, I was a wandering sort of man when it came to that, and once out of this fix, I'd wander again.

Come to think of it, there was nothing I'd rather be doing about then than just wandering, almost anywhere.

Surprising how proximity to a noose in the end of a rope can make man appreciate things. Living, just being alive, had never seemed quite so desirable as right now. When I started thinking of some of the fool chances I'd taken before I was dry behind the ears, it scared me . . . and did me no good at all. I was right here in these stone walls and time was closing in on me. Time was a noose.

"All right," I told Jane. "That there is a fool idea but it might work. My advice to you is to have an ace-in-the-hole, however, and get me a horse and saddle him up with a pistol on him and leave him in the trees back by Webster's stable."

She went out of there and Wesley put more water in my bucket. Wesley bothered me. That long tall boy had never done anyone any harm and I didn't want him out there when the shooting started.

Only two things I wanted. To get shut of this place and to put Sam Barlow in that grave at the Corners. And if I could pile Chance Thorne in there with him, I'd be more than pleased.

Belser? We don't worry about the Belsers of this world.

Once I was free he would scare himself to death thinking what I might do to him.

Standing by that window and looking out on the street I could see the red sun going down behind the old Tilden barn, and I could hear the squeaky complaints of a rusty pump as somebody pumped water for coffee or maybe for washing hands before supper.

I could smell food cooking, cabbage, it smelled like, and sometimes hear a door slam as somebody came or went. Standing there I heard the first sounds of somebody milking a cow into a tin pail. It was suppertime in Jefferson on the night before they were to hang Cullen Baker.

That was me. I was Cullen Baker, and I knew they planned to have that hanging tonight, and if they were right and I was wrong, this was the last sun I would ever see, the last of these sounds I'd hear.

Like a jackass braying, or an owl hooting . . . an owl? It was early for an owl.

More than one kind of owl hoot.

It was something to figure on, that hooting owl. Soon he hooted again. Time was shaping up, it soon would be hanging time and unless I wanted to be the key man at that hanging I would have to get out.

The streets were growing empty as folks went for supper. All right then, this was what I wanted. No use waiting until ten o'clock and maybe getting folks killed. Right now while everybody was busy with supper and when it wasn't quite dark, right now and without waiting any further. I didn't want Wesley to get hurt but I wasn't wanting to be hung, either. So I walked over to that door and took a good hold of those iron bars. Like I said, I'm a man of strength, and so I took hold of those bars and gave them a yank.

Nothing.

Just simply nothing at all. I took hold of those bars and braced myself and gave it everything I had . . . nothing.

That carpenter I'd said was slipshod, the one I figured hadn't bolted those two-by-sixes into the stone, he hadn't needed to. They were set so close and solid you could pull that wall down before they'd be noticed.

Right then I was scared. All the time I'd had it in mind that I could rip that doorframe out of there, I'd been sure of that—and nothing happened.

Sweat broke out on my forehead. That rope was suddenly mighty close. Sweat began to come out on me and it was cold sweat and my throat felt dry like nothing in this world. You could have bought my chances right then for a plugged two-bit piece and been ahead of the game. I felt like a limp deuce in an ace-high deck.

So I tried it again. Sometimes a man can be right stubborn, times like that, I spread my feet and braced them against the stone floor and gave a yank that would have taken a tree out by the roots . . . nothing.

Then I looked up at the ceiling. I don't know why. I was just exasperated and I raised a hand to swear and looked up—and I kept on looking up.

The ceiling of that cell was of spiked plank, nailed to four-by-fours which served as beams, and it was high, just beyond the reach of my fingers when I jumped to touch it.

Spiked to those beams. With how many spikes? And what was above that? A shake roof? Well, now! A man thinks of many things, and I thought of them all, but mostly I thought of getting out. Suddenly I looked out and the sun was gone, only a few lonely red and yellow steaks in a graying sky.

Time was short.

The window . . . it had to be deep because the walls were thick.

Reaching up I grasped those bars and pulled myself up. Getting a knee on the sill, I hoisted a foot, then balancing myself against a fall back into the room, I straightened up.

Standing on the floor that sill had been just an inch below eye-level for me, now, standing on the sill, I had to bend my knees to stand and bow my back against those planks in the ceiling. To hold the position I had to keep pressure on the planks, and if I relaxed I'd fall forward and would have to land on my feet on the floor to keep from being hurt.

But my back was against those planks, and my knees were bent. The chances were mighty good that the carpenter who fixed that door had done a job on these planks in the ceiling, but I would see. Using my hands to grip the top edge of the window behind me, I started to straighten out my legs. It was no go. I couldn't get enough pressure on it to make anything budge. Turning around and squatting on the ledge of the stone window I gripped a bar in one hand and started testing the ceiling planks with the other. And the second one I tried seemed the best chance. Turning and gripping a bar with one hand I put a shoulder against the plank and started to straighten my legs. Almost at once a nail screeched, but not too loudly. Waiting a moment and listening, I tried it again, and the plank gave still more. A third time and the spikes pulled free. There had been but two. With one hand I moved the board aside and then listened for an instant before I caught the edge of the adjoining board and pulled myself up and through the space.

It was completely black in the space under the roof, but I could feel the underside of the shakes. Swiftly I worked my way along, testing each one to the very rear of the building. And there I found one that was not tight. Tugging, I pulled the shake around and then got hold of another. There was an ear-splitting crack, and I caught my breath, and waited. Down below I heard footsteps that came to the rear of the jail, paused an instant, and then returned the way they had come.

At any minute someone might decide to check my cell, so there was nothing for it but to make the attempt now. Crawling through the hole, although it was a tight squeeze, I worked out onto the roof, slid down and then dropped from the eaves to the ground. Only an instant I hesitated, and then started to walk swiftly away toward Webster's stable.

There was about an acre of ground that must be crossed, and the lower end of the street. Trying not to look excited or do anything that would attract attention I walked from behind the building and crossed the street diagonally. Behind me a man came from the door of a house and I knew he was looking my way, but I simply continued to walk, but the hair on the back of my neck was crawling, and I wouldn't have given two cents for my chances right then.

Turning the corner I went into Webster's farmyard and crossed the yard toward the stable. Webster was a Union Leaguer, and very close to both Thorne and Belser, so I could expect no help from him if he came from the house and saw me. I could expect nothing but trouble, and lots of it.

The worst of it was, I had acted before I was expected and there might be no horse for me.

Quickly I trotted down the little slope into the trees and walked along the path where I expected the horse to be.

It was not there.

Turning I walked swiftly back along another way, searching the trees, but the area covered by trees was scarcely larger than a good sized farmyard, and the horse had to be within sight if he was there, but he wasn't.

And then I saw him.

The horse was not tied; he was walking toward me, ears pricked, reins dragging. At almost the same instant I heard a yell from the street, then a shout and loud voices arguing, swearing. They had discovered my escape.

There was no time left. I started for the horse and in almost the same breath the brush cracked and suddenly a torch flared up and then another.

The first person I saw was Chance Thorne, and he was grinning. The second was Joel Reese, but there were at least six, and they had rifles.

125

Caught!

Reese lowered his rifle and from around his waist he un-wrapped a short length of log chain.

Another man shucked a heavy belt with a large brass buckle, and several others had clubs. They stacked their guns and started for me.

"I've got the rope," Reese told me, "and when we get through you'll be glad to get it. Hanging will be a pleasure after this!"

They were all around me and they could see I was unarmed. Only I wasn't. Taking my time I tucked my thumbs behind my belt and stood looking around at them. "You've got it all your way, haven't you?" I asked. "But the first man who comes at me, I'll kill."

In the flickering light of the torch, and with them all unsus-pecting, they didn't see the slight movement when my thumb at the base of the derringer pushed it up into my palm.

Two bullets, and then they'd have me. I wanted Chance Thorne and I wanted Joel Reese.

"Lucky we caught that girl bringin' you the horse," Reese said. "A girl with a horse going down here at that time of night, well, it shaped up as suspicious. We followed a hunch."

The flickering torchlight danced on the cottonwood leaves, and under cover of the talk they had been edging in on me. I had the derringer in my hand and I was ready as a man can be.

There were guns on the horse, which was just outside the circle. There was a rifle, and at least one pistol, and there were full saddlebags and a blanket roll behind the saddle. I could kill two men and make a try for it, but there wasn't a chance that I'd make it. They had stacked their rifles, but each man I could see wore a belt gun—three of them, anyway.

That was three too many.

"All right," Chance said, "let's get him!"

Reese drew back his chain and they started for me and I fired. For the second time I missed Reese, but I hit the man holding the belt with the brass buckle. He screamed and the sound, coming with the gun blast, stopped them in their tracks.

"*Look out!*" It was Reese yelling. "He's got a *gun!*"

One man grabbed for a pistol and I fired again and hit him right in the belly and at the same instant there was a wild Texas yell from somewhere behind me and a voice that yelled, "Hold up, in there! Hold it!"

The yell was followed by a shot that knocked another man to the ground with a smashed hip. I knew that yell. It had to be Seth Rames.

From behind them another voice spoke. It was cool, easy, confident. It was John Tower. "That's right, boys. Just stand fast."

Turning abruptly I walked to the horse and stepped into the saddle, and when I had my hand on a pistol I turned on them. "If you've hurt that girl, I'll see every man of you buried in the swamps."

Somebody spoke up. "She's locked up at Reese's place."

"She isn't now," Tower replied. "She's gone, and I let her go, and if she's ever bothered again, I'll add my weight to Baker's."

They stood very still. Two voices had spoke but there might be more men. They were sure there were more, and I had no idea how many there were, only that I had a chance and suddenly the future was wide and bright again . . . if we could just ride out of here.

So I walked the horse to where Seth Rames was, and saw his big, raw-boned frame sitting a horse in the shadows.

"Stand fast!" he repeated, and then he swung his horse. On the soft earth it made almost no noise, but he rode along with me until we reached the highroad, and then he turned. He was a big man, as big as me in weight, but taller. "We'd better ride, Cullen. Tower's already gone."

We took out.

Riding at a good pace, I checked the rifle, and it seemed loaded. The pistol was okay, too. So we rode into the night.

Near the Corners, Seth drew up. "Got to reach the boys," he said, "and I've a soldier who'll let me through alone. You can make the swamps."

The roads were empty and still, and I knew them well. Luckily, I saw no one. Once I passed a house where a late light was shining, and near another a dog barked, but I rode on into the night with the cool damp air on my face, and the smell of the swamps. It was after midnight when I crossed the Louisiana state line heading for a place I knew on James Bayou.

Maybe they had expected me to keep going, to ride clear out of the country, but I wasn't about to go until I knew all my friends were safe. The place to which I was riding now was one nobody would connect me with, nobody knew I'd ever gone here, or had any friends here.

Avoiding Caddo Station I rode past the Salt Pits, and when daylight was gray in the sky I drew up near the dark bulk of a small cabin on the edge of the swamps. A dog barked, and a man came from the house and stood watching in my direction.

"It's Cullen, Mike, and I'm in trouble."

"Come on in."

Caddo Mike was a short, square man of powerful build, no longer young. This was solid ground, a little higher than most of it around here. Suddenly I realized this was one of the strange mounds that had been built here long before the oldest Indian could remember, and ages before the white man first came to the country.

Mike took my horse and dipped suddenly from sight. Following him I found him tying the horse in an underground stable concealed among the trees, and dug into the side of the mound. The stable walls were of ancient stone, built ages ago. There were four other horses, all fine animals. It was cool there, and quite pleasant. Caddo Mike had opened a skylight on a slope of the hill which he had covered with canvas. It allowed a little light.

"White men dig for gold," Mike explained, "long time ago, in the time of my grandfather. No gold. The Old People had no gold. Just bones here."

Caddo Mike's face was seamed and brown. I felt as if I had known him forever. When I was a boy, the first month we had been here from Tennessee we had found Caddo Mike staggering and delirious with fever on the edge of the swamp. We had taken him home, and dosed with quinine, he had survived to become our good friend.

One night he was in bed, and in the morning he was gone, but a few days later we found a haunch of venison hung from the porch, and on another morning, two fine wild turkeys. It had been Mike who taught me most of what I knew about the swamps where he had lived all his life. He was now, I guess, at least sixty. But he was strong and able to travel for miles on foot or horseback.

Mike made black coffee that was more than half chicory and laced it with rum. Then he brought out some corn pone, brown beans and venison.

In this remote corner Mike cultivated a field of corn, and a good-sized vegetable garden. He rarely went into any of the towns, and almost never to the same one twice in succession. White men as a rule he did not trust, and he avoided their questions or any contact with them other than involved in his few business transactions.

Over the food I explained to Mike all that had happened, and ended by telling him, "Mike, I need to know what happened back there. And I must get a message to Katy Thorne."

When Mike had ridden away I stretched out on the bed with a pistol at my side, and trusting to the dogs who were wary of strangers, I slept.

In the late afternoon I awakened suddenly, and for a moment, as always when I awaken, I lay still, listening. There was no sound, so swinging my feet to the floor I padded across to the window and peered out into a sun-bright world.

Going out back I dipped a bucket in the tank and sloshed water over myself. The water was cold and it felt good. Four more buckets and I began to feel human and alive, so I dried off in the sun and then went back in and dressed.

First off I checked my guns. There had been a pistol on the horse and Mike had offered me another which I accepted. The rifle was my own Spencer, although how Jane Watson came by it I don't know and can't guess unless John Tower got it somehow.

It was a hot, still afternoon. There were a few scattered clouds.

Locating the feed bin I fed Mike's chickens, and then the horses. Somewhere out on the bayou a loon called, a lonesome sound. Returning to the cabin I sliced a chunk from a ham and fried up some ham and eggs, and made coffee.

The sun was low by the time I finished eating and I was growing restless. Mike was not about to be back so soon, so I rummaged around for something to read. Right now I might as well admit I'm not much of a reader. I make out to read most things, given time, but I've got to have time and quiet.

Caddo Mike, whom I never figured to read at all, had a sight of old magazines and books around, most of them mighty old. There was a magazine there, a copy of *Atlantic Monthly* for August, 1866, and I started reading a piece in it called "A Year in Montana."

Reading that article, I'd nearly finished when I dozed off and awakened to find myself scared . . . I'd no business sleeping so sound or so much. And me with the light burning. Putting out the light I stood in the door until my eyes were right and then stepped out. One of the dogs came up and stood near me, and I spoke to him, mighty soft. His tail thumped my leg, and I walked down off the stoop.

The night was too quiet to suit me, edgy the way I was, and

I walked out away from the cabin and turned to look back. A man could have stood where I was, within sixty feet of the house, day or night, and never known it was there.

Near Caddo Mike's the bayou described one of those loops so common among bayous, and even in the main stream of the Sulphur, which was well north of here. The bayou took a loop and then doubled back until it almost met itself, and at this point it was shallow and almost choked with hyacinth and old logs. The road at this point followed the outside of the loop, going up one side around the end and down the other side. Nervous as a bobcat about to have kittens, I crossed one arm of the bayou and started across toward the trail on the other side. Yet I'd gone not thirty feet when I heard riders.

Stopping dead still, I heard a voice grumbling, then another ordering silence. That grumbling voice was the Barlow man whom Katy had nursed, and this must be the Barlow crowd!

Listening, straining my ears to hear, I then heard someone ask a question of someone called Sam . . . and it figured to be Barlow himself.

They had drawn up, stopping on the road that cut me off from a return to Caddo Mike's. Did they know of him and his place? Had they caught Mike, and were they now searching for me?

No! Mike would die before he would talk, and there was no connection between us that anyone could figure out.

Nevertheless, I started on, moving across the narrow neck toward the other side. When I was on the inside bank of the bayou and hunting a place to cross its fifteen yards of water, at this point a fairly deep pool and clear of growth I heard another party of riders.

Squatting on my heels, I waited.

This party was walking their horses and from the jingle of accoutrements could only be a party of soldiers.

The neck of land I had crossed was barely a hundred yards

131

from bayou to bayou, but it was all of a half mile around the loop by following the road. The idea came to me suddenly.

Calling out in a low but clear voice, just loud enough for them to hear me, I said, "You fellers huntin' Cullen Bakuh, you better cut an' run! He's a-comin' raht down the road toward you all, an' he's sure set for trouble!"

"Who's there?" The voice had a sharp, military ring that I hoped couldn't be heard on the Barlow side. "Come out and show yourself!"

By that time I was moving back toward the other side. I wanted to get to Caddo Mike's and a horse just as fast as I could make it. If all went the way I hoped, all hell was going to break loose any time within the next fifteen minutes or less.

Barlow's boys had moved on when I reached the far side, but I was only in the middle of a log, crossing the bayou, when I heard a voice ring out, "Hey, there! Who's that?" And a moment later a ringing command, *"Fire!"*

There had been at least a dozen men in the Army command, and probably twice that many.

The blast of gunfire smashed into the night's stillness like a breaking of a gigantic tree limb, and like it was followed by a deafening silence.

The silence lasted a moment only, then there was a rattle of gunfire, a quick exchange of shots, shots, yells and then more silence.

On the edge of the bayou I started to cross the road, then heard a rush of horses' hoofs and a man riding. He pulled up, listening for sounds of pursuit. And then I heard someone running. He fell, scrambled up and came on, his breath coming in great gasps.

The man on the horse started, then stopped and walked his horse slowly back up the road.

"Bravo?" By the gasping breath it was the running man.

"Sam, anybody else make it?"

"Ed, I think Ed did. He dove into the swamp."

132

"The rest all gone?"

"Every man-jack of them."

Carefully, I eased myself across the road, then waited a bit. Sam Barlow was a man could stand some talking to, but shooting right now would bring the Army down on us, and I'd no wish to be captured again . . . I'd come too close to stretching my neck as it was.

"Somebody set us up like pigeons," Barlow was saying.

"Thorne, he figures he don't need us no longer."

"No, not Thorne," Barlow replied, but he didn't sound very convinced.

"Let's get out of here," Bravo suggested. "Come daylight they'll shake this patch down like they was huntin' coons. We better be far off come daylight."

There was no sign of Mike at the cabin. Packing up some grub, I slipped away from the cabin and hid in the brush near the hidden stable. From where I lay I could observe the cabin and the road approaching it. The way I saw it I needed to talk to Mike before I moved, I needed to know whatever he'd found out about the others. There was no possibility of going home now, and somehow I wasn't sorry. Both Lacy and Katy had been right all along, for they'd give me no chance here. Out West, well I could find a place for myself and make my own way, maybe in the mines or the cattle business. Maybe I could, with Katy's help, even learn to read and write better and make something of myself.

With Katy's help? I blushed there in the darkness. Who was I to think a girl like that would go on the dodge with me? The more I thought of it the more I figured she did indeed like me. But maybe I was wrong, and I'd no right to ask her, anyway.

To go West I had to go through the country I'd just come out of, or skirt around it, which was mighty near as bad, so whatever Mike could tell me would help. But most of all, I had to know those who helped me got clear; it just wasn't in me to go scot-free and leave a friend in the lurch.

Suddenly two riders came down the trail and drew up nearby, far enough away to hear them talking. "Why waste our time? No matter what the sergeant says, they're gone. That wasn't Cullen Baker, anyway, that was the Barlow crowd. You think I don't know that bunch? I used to run in the Thickets my ownself."

There was a mutter of voices I could hear, and then the first man spoke out again. "Six Barlow men dead and nine wounded or captured. It was a good haul."

"Who d'you suppose that was who yelled at us?"

The first soldier chuckled. "Who d'you suppose?"

When daylight came again I went to the stable to saddle up, but before I could get the saddle on the horse, I heard the dogs barking and knew from the sound they were welcoming someone they knew.

It was Caddo Mike. And he was alone.

SEVEN

Rifle cradled in the hollow of my arm, I stepped from among the trees.

"You got to git from here."

"Did you see Miss Katy?"

"You know Willow Bluff? West of the old ferry in Bowie County? She gonna meet you there."

Few people lived in that remote pine-covered area across the Sulphur, and there was a chance to reach the place unobserved. And it was on the way out of the country where I was known.

"She shouldn't be riding there alone."

"I don't figure she gonna be alone." Caddo Mike did not enlarge upon the statement, but went on, "They huntin' you. The sodgers huntin' you, the sodgers huntin' Sam Barlow, Sam Barlow huntin' you."

"What about Bob Lee?"

"He had a runnin' fight with sodgers. Joe Tinney, he dead. Buck ride back to pick him up, he dead."

It would be like Buck to ride back for his brother. It was the end for them all. The feeling was on me that I would never reach Willow Bluff, nor see Katy again. Their luck had played out.

The urge was on me to ride into Jefferson and kill Chance Thorne. Deeply, bitterly, I felt he was the cause of all that had happened, and that until he died there could be no peace for me, no matter where I went or what I did. Had it not been for his hatred of me Bob Lee and Bickerstaff might now be at peace with the Union Leaguers.

No, that was untrue. They were men who would fight and alone if need be, for whatever they believed. They were men who got their backs up at tyranny.

"You ride careful, ride skeery," Mike advised. "They bad people."

Mike insisted I take his dapple-gray mare, and she was a good horse, a better horse than Jane Watson had found for me. Still, I was wishing I had that ornery buckskin mule of mine. He could eat a handful of grass, drink a cupful of water, and he was already to go again.

Stepping into the saddle I looked down at Mike, reluctant to leave. "S'long, Mike," I said, and walked the horse away, not looking back.

From this point every step was a danger, every mile an added risk. Right then I was sure I was going to be killed, it was a feeling I had not had before, and one that I could not shake. I should never have returned after the war, but to abandon the land would take all the meaning from the years of labor Pa and Ma had put in. Come to think of it, Pa himself had moved on a couple of times, and in such a case, he would move, too.

The mare was a good one with an urge to travel. She stepped out with her ears pricked forward like she knew she was going into new country, like she wanted to see what was beyond the hill and around the bend. This was a traveling mare.

So north we rode, away from Jefferson, away from Caddo Lake. I was in Louisiana with the Arkansas line somewhere to the north and the Texas line just to the west, only a few miles away. When I crossed into Texas I would be in Cass County, which was my home county, but I had just to hope that I'd see nobody who knew me. After crossing Baker Creek, I turned west.

Avoiding roads I kept to old trails the Caddoes used and that Cherokee hunting parties had used when they came down from the Nation. When I forded the river and rode up to Mush Island I took it almighty cautious to see before I was seen.

A broken branch with green leaves lay across the path ahead of me, so I walked the mare along until I saw the three stones beside the trail. The triangle they formed pointed into the woods.

They were signs our outfit used, but they might also be a trap, so I reined the mare over and hooted like an owl, waited, then hooted again.

After a minute or so a frog sounded back in the woods, and only Matt Kirby could do it so natural-like.

So I sat my horse and kept my eyes open for trouble, and waited for him to come up to me, but when he came he had a stranger with him. "It's all right," Kirby said. "This here's a cousin to Buck and Joe. I know him."

The stranger was as large as either Kirby or me, and he was almost in rags.

Mike had said Katy was bringing some clothes to their meeting at Willow Bluff so I dug into my saddlebags. "You could use a shirt," I said, and hauled out my old checkered shirt and a pair of homespun jeans made by a Mormon woman near Cove Fort. They were none too good but better than what the fellow had on. "You take these," I said, "I've had my wear out of them."

"Thanks." The big fellow was mighty embarrassed. "I'm

beholden. We uns are fresh out of cash money up on the Red.
Man gits mahty little for his crops nowadays."

"What are you down this way for?"

He looked up, honest surprise on his face. "Why, they kilt
my cousins. Somebody kills our'n, we kill them. That's the way
it is up on the Red."

"You go home," I told him, "you just go back up there.
You'll catch nothing but trouble down here."

"I got it to do," he said soberly. "Pa says so an' I got a feelin'
he's raht. Them Tinney boys. I growed up with Buck an' Joe.
Can't hear of them bein' laid away without the men who kilt
'em laid away, too."

"You go home," I insisted.

Bob Lee came up through the woods, Longley a length
behind, and both of them grinned when they saw me. "Figured you for swamp bait," Bob said, "figured they'd tacked up
your hide."

"Take some doing," I said.

"Bickerstaff went to Johnson County."

We squatted on our heels and talked commonplaces while
Kirby and his new partner rustled wood and started some
coffee. Bob Lee looked tired and even Longley, the youngest
of the lot except for this new man, looked beat. Bob Lee, he
looked around us. "I never liked this place; makes a man
spooky."

"You going to Mexico?"

"Uh-huh. I figure to ranch down there." Bob Lee took the
broken stub of a cigar from his pocket. "Down in Chihuahua I
have friends. I'll send for the wife later."

"I'm riding West."

It was on us now, the feeling that we were leaving was riding
us, and a man could feel the uneasiness among us. All of us had
been riding elbow to elbow with death for months, and yet
now that we had a chance to get out we were more scared than
ever.

I never figured it was a cowardly thing to be scared. It's to be scared and still to face up to what scares you that matters. A man in our way of life faces guns many times, and he knows a gun can kill, but now we had our chance to get out and away and we were ready. No sense in prolonging it. Taking the coffee Matt offered me I drank a mouthful. "I'm pulling out," I said. "I'm getting shut of this place."

Lee glanced up at me as I straightened up. Longley got up, too. Matt poked at the fire, and the youngster sat there and looked at us like he couldn't understand. All of us knew that we weren't about to see each other again, and we had shared troubles.

"Wait a spell," Lee told me, "and I'll ride as far as Fannin County with you."

My clothes itched me and I felt cold and lonely. A little wind came through the trees and I shivered. The feeling was on me that there was death in this place and it was my death that was coming. "Bob, I wouldn't go to Fannin County if I were you."

"I've got to see the wife."

"Don't go! Write to her. You light out for Mexico and don't stop until you've got Laredo behind you. I'm telling you, Bob, we should all get shut of Texas. You ride out, Bob, and you keep going. You're a good man, one of the best I ever knew, and there's no sense you spilling blood of yours for a cause that wasted itself away. You keep riding."

"Never saw you jumpy before."

Turning around I looked at that long, tall, handsome Bill Longley. "You hang up your guns, Bill. They'll get you killed, believe me."

"A man has to die," he said.

Holding out my hand to Bob, I said, "So long, Bob. Easy riding."

"Adios, compadre."

Longley got up. He looked awkward and embarrassed. "See you out West sometime. You watch for me."

139

"I'll do that."

Throwing the rest of my coffee into the dead leaves I looked into the empty cup, then I turned and dropped the cup and stepped into the saddle. For a long moment I sat my saddle unmoving, my back turned to them, for we all knew it was the last time, and the sickness of leaving was on me. Then I rode away.

"He should have waited to eat," Longley said.

Kirby glanced up. "A doom's on him, can't you see it? My old grandma told me when the doom's on a man and he knows he's going to die, he's like that."

"That's fool talk." Bob Lee dropped his cup. "I'm not waiting. I'm riding to Fannin County. Coming Bill?"

When they were gone the tall young man rubbed his eyes and looked sheepishly at Kirby. "You sleepy? I'm raht tard."

Only a few yards away I'd stopped again, almost afraid to go on, yet feeling like Bob Lee that there was something about this place that gave me a bad feeling. I'd sat there, listening to them talk, hearing the retreating sounds of the horses of Lee and Longley, and then I heard Kirby say, "Sleep, I'll wake you to take watch when I'm sleepy."

So I rode away under the trees, sitting easy in the saddle and shaped up for a long ride West.

At daybreak I was still riding, but the mare was dead tired and we both needed rest. There was plenty of time to get to Willow Bluff—but that was the trouble. A man always thought there was plenty of time, and there never was.

When I awakened and pulled on my boots I checked my guns and then scouted around. By the sun I judged I'd slept a couple of hours, and after a scout around I put together a small fire in a hollow place near a tree where the rising smoke could lose itself in the branches, and made coffee. Broiling a chunk of beef, I took a couple of swallows of coffee and then with the beef in my left hand, taking occasional bites, I strolled over to where the trail went through the trees.

There was no evidence that the trail had been used by anyone else, although I saw where an inquisitive deer had been checking my tracks. This was an old Caddo trail, and kept to high ground under the trees, dipping only occasionally to lonely springs or to the river. The days of Caddo wandering were almost a thing of the past, so the trail was unused. It was the same trail I'd taken out of the country once before. My camp was south of the Sulphur near Whiteoak Creek.

Both Barlow and the soldiers would be hunting me now. I'd escaped from prison now, and for that alone they'd be after me. But I was out of Cass County, and pretty much beyond Barlow's zone of action.

There was a mockingbird doing tricks in a treetop some distance away, but no other sound. At the fire I finished eating, finished my coffee and put out the fire with great care. I'd seen too much damage done by carelessly put out fires, or those left burning by some damn' fool.

It was a lazy, sunlit morning, and I was about three miles from Willow Bluff. In the silent woods a sound can be heard from quite a distance, so when I heard a sound I straightened up and listened.

It could have been a branch breaking, but animals do not break branches, and if broken deliberately it must be for a cooking fire. If otherwise, then somebody was sneaking around and I wasn't ready for that.

Moving easy-like, I saddled up and put my stuff together. Mounting up I walked the horse off under the trees, keeping away from my lonely little trail until some distance from the night camp. The main trail, such as it was, was several miles away, but there was another used occasionally that would touch at Willow Bluff. There was not a chance in a million anyone would guess my trail was here. Fact is, it would take a sharp man, just stumbling on it, to judge it a trail at all.

At no time had I failed to practice the technique of drawing a gun fast. Each day except when in jail I'd spent some time

141

working at it, and I knew I'd become a sight faster than when I killed Dud Butler in Fort Worth. Accuracy had never been a problem. From boyhood I'd been skillful with all sorts of weapons.

At intervals I drew up to judge the silence of the woods, to sort out the sounds, and the closer I was to final escape the more jumpy I became. The very fact that I was getting out made every move more careful because I wanted nothing to go wrong at the last minute.

About noontime I rode down to the bank of the Sulphur. It was a dangerous river, many ways. Under the surface there was an entangling mass of roots, old snags, and masses of dead and long-submerged water lilies, sudden shallows or depths. The old ferry was several miles downstream, and the place where I now sat my saddle was an old Caddo crossing almost two miles upstream from Willow Bluff.

Approaching the bluff from the north seemed a likely idea, and I'd circled around, cutting for sign, and checking the country. Right about then I'd an uneasy feeling the woods weren't at all empty. Could be I was jumpy, but the feeling was on me.

Katy might come at any time, and she might not be alone, so I'd want to check whoever was with her before I showed up in plain sight. Also, there was always the chance she'd been followed. A man on the dodge can't rule out anything as unlikely. Walking the dapple into the water I waded him and swam him across the Sulphur.

The old trail divided here and a branch went northwest toward a couple of shacks called White Cotton. The other branch went northeast to intersect with a very poor trail running north to Dalby Springs and southeast toward the ferry. Turning off the trail before it reached the road, I worked a cautious way through the forest toward Willow Bluff.

Willow Bluff was one of several bluffs that were actually little more than high banks covered with willows as was much of this bottom in 1869. On the edge of a thicket near some pines I got down from the saddle. There was no reason I could think of for feeling like I did, but there was panic in me. The silence of the forest was suddenly oppressive and I had to fight back an urge to climb into the saddle and light out of there and run like I never had in my life until I was far from here, far from Texas, and far from anything I ever knew.

Easing the girth on the dapple I squatted on my heels and lighted my pipe, and then I stayed right there, listening, making myself easy. The earth smelled of decayed leaves and rotting timber. Along a fallen log walked a big red ant, and a bumblebee bumbled lazily among the wild flowers—no other sound came through the trees.

Below me and to the right was Willow Bluff. There was a tumbled-down log cabin lurched half over like a sorry old drunk. There was a well, the remains of a pole corral and some unfinished fence, and not far off was the north bank of the Sulphur. I could hear the water running through the branches of a huge old tree that had fallen off the bank into the stream.

There was some open meadow down there, and from where I squatted on the slope I could see it all without being seen. A fly buzzed in the sunshine, my horse cropped grass, down on the river a fish jumped. Easing my pistols in my belt I knocked out the pipe on the palm of my hand.

Nothing moved anywhere, yet my stomach felt empty and I felt touchy as a boar with a sore snout. There was no sense to feeling this way: Katy would be here soon.

When they came it wasn't like I expected. Katy was there, but with her was Lacy Petraine and John Tower, and they were leading a pack horse. Tower got down from the horse and helped the two girls down, but I sat right still and didn't move.

Impatient as I was, I sat right still, just waiting and listening. If they had been followed, I wanted to know it. When ten minutes had passed I could wait no longer, so cinching up the gray, I walked down the slope.

"*Cullen!*" Katy ran toward me. "We heard you were dead! Warren said he'd killed you!"

It made no kind of sense. Not at first. Seems when they were well on their way they had spotted a rider coming toward them, and when he pulled up it was Warren and he was wild, and he was yelling, "*I killed him! I killed him!*"

"Killed who?" Tower had demanded.

"I killed that outlaw!" Warren was excited and his eyes had a glassy shine. "*I killed Cullen Baker!*"

"You killed Cullen Baker?" Tower had asked. "A sneaking little pipsqueak like you?"

"Don't you dare talk to me like that!" Warren's voice was shrill. "Don't you dare! *I* killed Cullen Baker!"

"I don't believe you," Tower had said. "You're out of your mind."

Warren had laughed, and Katy said she was shocked by his manner. He acted as if he were intoxicated. There was a queerness about him, an almost sadistic excitement that revolted them.

"Oh, I killed him all right! He thought he was so much! He was there in the brush with another fellow. I shot them both. Cullen was lying there in the checkered shirt he always wore and he never knew what happened. That other man, the one called Kirby, he started to get up, and—"

"You shot him when he was *asleep?*" Tower's face was white with fury, Katy said. "Why you little—"

"He didn't kill him, Mr. Tower," Katy said. "I just know he didn't."

Warren had turned on her, almost white with anger. "You fool! Can't you see now? He's dead! He's dead now, and nothing but a clod of empty flesh! And *I* killed him! *I!* There's no sense you mooning around over him. It will be me they talk about now. I'll be *the man who killed Cullen Baker!*"

"I think," Tower had said, "I think I'll kill him."

"No," Katy stopped him, "he doesn't understand. Down

144

here," she said, looking at Warren, "a man is admired for daring to face another armed man with a pistol and for settling his quarrels bravely. It isn't a killing that is admired, it is the courage to fight for what you believe. You won't be admired as the man who killed Cullen Baker, you will be despised as someone who murdered a sleeping man."

They had turned then and ridden away as he stared after them. And the last thing they heard was a contemptuous laugh, but it was a hollow sound.

"I won't believe it," Katy had said, "I'm going on to Willow Bluff."

And in the end they had all come on along.

So there we stood in the warm sunshine of the meadow, with the grass around our feet and a blue sky overhead with a few white puffballs of fleecy cloud drifting. We heard the gurgle of the water around that fallen tree, and I looked at Katy and she looked at me and I knew my home was going to be wherever she was, that I didn't need the land Pa had owned, that I didn't need anything, anywhere as long as I had her.

Tower, he turned to Lacy, and he said, "Something I've got to say. Lacy, I love you. I'm in Texas because I came hunting you, because I had to find you. I think I've loved you ever since you were Terry's wife, but Lacy, I didn't want to kill him, I didn't want to at all."

Right then Katy was in my arms and I wasn't thinking about anything else but I heard Lacy say, "John, I think we should go West, too."

And Katy was saying to me that she'd brought Sandoval for me, and then I looked up and threw Katy away from me.

Chance Thorne and Sam Barlow were there at the edge of the woods, just beyond the old well. And there were two others with them.

145

Four men standing in a scattered line, and they had us covered.

Fifteen feet away from me John Tower was facing them also.

"John," I said quietly, "it looks like we're going to do some shooting."

We both knew what could happen to the girls if we were killed without them.

"I'll take Barlow and Thorne, John," I told him, speaking low. "You get those others."

"All right, but you're getting all the best of it."

Sam Barlow was grinning. "Wish we were closer to that grave you dug for me. I figured you to fill it."

"John"—they were walking nearer—"I've been working on something. Getting my gun out fast, shooting from where it is, it worked against Butler in Fort Worth."

"I saw it."

"Takes them a moment to think, you know."

"All right."

They had come up within thirty feet of us now, and Chance was looking at Katy, and there was nothing nice in the way he looked. "You always despised me," Chance said, "and whatever happens here, nobody knows. Nobody will ever know."

"I'd like to take time to set fire to you, Cullen," Barlow was saying, "but we don't want to keep them girls a-waitin'. They'll be impatient for some real men, seems like, so we're goin' to kill you."

"Sam." I was cold inside. I felt like ice. I could feel the sun and hear a mockingbird in the trees and I could see the wasps hovering about the well. "Sam," I said, "there's one thing I've got to tell you."

"Yeah? What's th—"

The brief lightning of my shot coming against men who believed themselves securely in command stabbed across the afternoon.

The months of hard practice, speeded now by the knowledge

146

of waiting death. With complete coolness I fired a second shot into Barlow, then swung the gun muzzle and as a bullet blasted past me, a shot touched off by panic, I shot Chance Thorne through the body. My fourth bullet went through Chance's neck under his ear and drenched the falling man with his own blood.

I stepped around the well toward Barlow. Tower had to do what he must, these two were mine.

Barlow was trying to get up. He knew he had bought it. He knew what a bullet through the stomach could do and he had two of them right where he lived. He was dying and he wanted only one thing, to hurt me and to take me with him.

"They got Bob Lee," he gasped at me. "He was ridin' from his home to Mexico when the Peacocks ambushed him." He gasped hoarsely, sweat standing out on his forehead. "They got Bickerstaff over in Alvarado. Now I'm gettin' you."

He turned the gun muzzle on me and I kicked it from his hand, then I glanced over at Chance.

Thorne was twisting on the bloody grass, dying in the sunlight of a warm afternoon in Texas. "I wish . . . I wish . . ." Whatever he wished none of us knew, for he died there on the grass looking up at the empty sky through the leaves of the oak that stood by the well.

"It worked, Cullen," Tower said. "I'd never have believed it."

Lacy was ripping his shirt sleeve where a bullet had cut through the deltoid muscle of his shoulder.

"Warren said he had killed you," Katy said, "and if you don't appear again, it will be believed, so let Cullen Baker die. Take another name, in another place."

We switched saddles so I could ride Sandoval and Katy the dappled mare. This much of the dream remained, that we had a stallion and a mare, and it was a beginning for any man, and most of all, I'd come up out of it with Katy Thorne.

So we mounted up and rode away in the sunlight, four of the living who left four of the dead behind.

And that was the way of it, although down along the Sulphur and the bayous around Lake Caddo some will say that Cullen Baker was an unreconstructed rebel who carried on a lone fight, and those who read a book written by Thomas Warren will tell you that Cullen was a drunken murderer and a thief. Only that was not the end. . . .

A man can breed horses and cattle and still find time to read, even to study law of an evening when he has a wife to help and encourage him, and for a man with an education the world is a wide place and the opportunities are many, but the old habits and ways are not forgotten and on my desk today there lies a Dragoon Colt, polished, cleaned and loaded to remind me of the days along the bayous when I invented the first fast draw.

Tonight John Tower will drive out from town and we will walk down to the corrals together to watch the horses, two tall old men who long ago stood side by side in a green sunlit meadow on the banks of the Sulphur River, but that was long, long ago, and in another world than this, another time.